365
Stories for Bedtime

© 1984 Schwager & Steinlein
English Language Edition, designed and produced by
Autumn Publishing Limited, Chichester, England.
Translation by Ruth Foulkes

Published in this edition by Galley Press, an imprint
of W H Smith & Son Limited
Registered No 237811 England
Trading as WHS Distributors, St. John's House,
East Street, Leicester, LE1 6NE

Typeset by Avonset, Midsomer Norton, Bath, England
Printed in Italy
ISBN 0 86136 885 1

365 Stories for Bedtime

Rosaline's Plant

Rosaline, the caterpillar, was sunbathing on her sun bed next to her favourite plant. She watched over the plant carefully so that no-one would take it away from her.

The plant was fully grown now but when it was a baby, Rosaline had looked after it very carefully; she had watered it regularly and weeded the soil around the plant. Now that it was fully grown Rosaline loved to sun herself by it and enjoyed it when beetles, snails and other caterpillars came by and admired the plant. Rosaline was indeed very proud of her plant, but she was not selfish; for whenever she heard of a sick animal she would take honey and pollen from the plant to the animal, to help it get better quickly.

Horace and Morris

Have you heard of the two dwarves called Horace and Morris? Well, it's time to get to know them now. I shall tell some stories about them in the next few pages.

One day, Horace and Morris were walking through the meadow when they came across a lovely shiny, red apple in the long grass.

"Hey!" cried Horace joyfully, "we can make some juice from this apple and throw a party for all our friends."

Morris thought this was a great idea and so the two dwarves began to think up ways of getting the heavy apple home.

"I know," said Morris, "we can get two mice to push the apple home for us." And that is just what they decided to do.

They soon found two helpful mice and they promised the mice that they could come to the party if they helped them get the apple home.

In the meantime darkness had fallen and a glow-worm kindly lit the way for them. When they reached home the dwarves thanked their helpers and said that as soon as the apple juice was ready they would receive an invitation to the party.

Party Preparations

Whilst Horace was busy brewing the apple juice, Morris sat down at a toadstool to write out all the invitations on light green leaves. Indeed, when you have as many friends as Horace and Morris it takes a long time to write out party invitations.

Everyone was to be invited: the two mice, the birds, the beetles, the ladybirds, the hedgehog, the frog, the squirrel, the snails, the rabbit, and not forgetting all the other dwarves and elves.

When Morris had finished all the invitations he wondered where he would find a postman to deliver them. Just then, the snail came by and offered to hand out the invitations. Morris laughed and said, "Oh no, you'd be too slow, by the time you'd delivered them, the Summer would be over!"

At that moment, a rabbit hopped by and Morris called out to the rabbit, "Hello there, you've come at the right moment, how would you like to deliver all the party invitations for me?" "I'd love to," said the rabbit. "Am I invited too?" he asked. "Of course you are," said Morris, and so the rabbit set off as postman.

Looking for Musicians

"Our party can begin now," said Horace when the apple juice was ready.

Morris however had realised that they had all forgotten something very important — the music!

"A party without music is like bread without butter!" said Morris. "Where-ever will we find a musical band around here?" said Horace. "Let's think this over for a few minutes."

Horace sat by his favourite tree stump and put his index finger on his nose, because that is how he could think best. Morris stood on his head on the damp grass because that's how he could think best. For a while there was complete silence.

"I've got it!" shouted both dwarves together and then they roared with laughter as they both had the same idea. "We can ask the frog with the loud croak to go and search for some musicians for us," they said together.

The two dwarves jumped up and set off to the pond to find Gordon the friendly frog. When they found Gordon they told him about the problem they had, and he agreed that a party without music was no fun at all. So he promised that he would start looking for musicians the very next day.

The Music Rehearsal

Early the next morning, Gordon the frog told the two dwarves that the musicians which he had found were on their way to meet them.

Just then, a cuckoo flew by and said, "If you need my voice at all I shall gladly join the band."

Later on, three nightingales appeared, who sang beautifully. Then a woodpecker came by who could beat time perfectly.

A fairy flew down with a harp under her arm, and a fat, merry dwarf brought an accordian with him. When a hedgehog came along with a drum, Horace and Morris were speechless with amazement.

They asked Gordon the frog to be the conductor, and suggested he organize a rehearsal. Gordon wasted no time and called out, "Attention everyone, after three, play the 'Forest Waltz', one, two, three . . ." The band began to play and the waltz sounded lovely. Horace and Morris jumped for joy and cried out, "What a wonderful party it will be with such good music!"

The musicians rehearsed for a long time and it was night when they left.

"See you tomorrow at the party, and many thanks," called Horace and Morris after them.

Party Time

The day of the party was warm and sunny. Horace and Morris got up bright and early as there were still a lot of things to be done.

Horace hung lanterns on the branches of the trees. Morris set out logs for the guests to sit on when they were too tired to dance any more.

Then they put out the beakers for the apple juice on a large toadstool and Horace put on an apron, as he was going to serve the drinks.

Morris, on the other hand, would welcome the guests to the party and would see that they all enjoyed themselves.

A group of dwarves with seven pretty fairies were the first guests to arrive; the rabbit and his family were the next; then the two mice; the hedgehog and the bees.

Everyone who had been invited had come to the party.

The musicians arrived on time and at long last, after all the preparations, the party could begin!

The sun was just setting and the evening was warm — just perfect for a party.

Party Continued

Gordon, the frog, waved his baton and the band played a loud fanfare, and at once there was silence.

Morris called out, "My dear friends, I heartily welcome you all to our party and wish you a wonderful evening! Horace has brewed some excellent apple juice and Gordon and the musicians will play music that you can dance to, so enjoy yourselves."

Whilst everyone was still quiet, Morris carried on with his little speech. "Horace and I would also like to thank those of you who helped us with the arrangements and preparations for this party," he said.

When the band began to play, everyone started to dance. Mr Hedgehog asked his wife to dance, Rabbit swirled round and round with an enchanting fairy, and four dwarves all danced in a ring. Everyone was singing, laughing, dancing and happily chattering.

Horace poured out the apple juice, and when it got dark Morris lit the lanterns and the glow-worms also helped to light up the party with their small lanterns.

So the party went on, until something unforgettable happened, but I shall tell of that in the next story.

Where is Peter?

When the party was in full swing, a dwarf came running up to Morris and said breathlessly, "Peter has disappeared, I can't find him anywhere."

"Calm down," said Morris, "we'll soon find him, don't worry." Morris beckoned to a glow-worm to go with him to search for the dwarf known as Peter.

He wasn't amongst the dancers, nor was he at the toadstool bar, nor was he sitting on the logs — where-ever was he then? "Peter, where are you," shouted Morris. How would Peter hear him above all this noise? The band would have to stop playing for a short while.

Then Morris shouted again and this time he heard a faint voice saying, "Over here," and as he went towards the tall oak tree, he saw Peter sitting beneath it, holding his tummy.

"I feel so awful I think I'm going to die," groaned Peter. Morris bent down and said to Peter, "Don't be silly, you're not going to die, you've just drunk too much apple juice, that's all. I'll bring you a cup of herb tea and you'll soon feel better."

A Wet Surprise

Peter drank the herb tea and soon felt much better. The party went on and the guests enjoyed the dancing.

Just then, Morris felt a drop of water on his nose. He looked up to the sky and said, "Oh no! It's going to rain, just when the party was really going well." No sooner had he said that, than it started to pour down with rain.

The guests ran for cover, under the shelter of the toadstools, squealing and shrieking as they hurried. Some of them even took shelter beneath thick tree roots and large stones.

The band fled into the dwarves' house and carried on playing cheerfully so that everyone could hear the music whilst they were sheltering.

Gordon, the frog, however, remained in the middle of the dance floor and got thoroughly wet. He loved the rain more than anything else in the world. This was the best thing that could happen for him. This jolly party and all the fun, and rain too! He thought he was the luckiest frog alive!

The Party Ends

The rain stopped almost as quickly as it had begun. The raindrops shone like diamonds in the moonlight and all the dwarves, animals and fairies thought this quite beautiful. They could hardly take their eyes off the twinkling raindrops.

They sat down in a circle and sang lots of merry songs.

The apple juice had all gone and they were far too tired to dance any more. The party was over.

The guests thanked Horace and Morris for a wonderful evening and then they set off home, with the glow-worms lighting the way for them.

Soon it was as quiet as any other night in the wood. The stars shone and the wind blew gently in the trees as the dwarves slept in their moss beds, dreaming of the party and all the fun they had had that evening with their friends. They all had very sweet dreams that night and hoped they could have fun like that again, soon!

Clearing Up

The two dwarves had a long lie in the next morning and did not get up until nearly lunch time. They both groaned at the thought of tidying up after the party — it was such a mess!

But they soon set to work — Horace collected together all the beakers that were lying around whilst Morris took down the lanterns from the trees. Later Horace swept the floor and as he did so he found lots of bits and pieces that guests had left behind: Gordon's baton, a dwarf's shoe and a hat, to name but a few articles.

"We shall take good care of these things until our friends can come and collect them," said Morris. A little later Rabbit appeared and joined in the clearing up. Soon the work was done and Rabbit stayed to chat with the dwarves and to enjoy a well-earned pipe. "Let's have another party next year," said the dwarves and Rabbit added, "Yes, let's!"

Tim, the centipede, had lived quite happily for a long time under a large stone. He had fed on small plants and leaves and nothing had disturbed his peaceful life.

One day, however, he had a great yearning to go on a long journey. He might even be able to combine it with going to see distant relatives such as Uncle Fred and Cousin John, he thought.

For such a journey he would need strong hard-wearing shoes, so he decided to go to the Cobbler's. This particular Cobbler had made very good shoes for all kinds of animals — dainty black velvet shoes for lady birds, green ballet shoes for grasshoppers, small red leather boots for beetles and solid working shoes for the dung beetles. The Cobbler worked very hard, often well into the night because he had no-one to help him.

Tim told the Cobbler that he needed 100 shoes for his 100 feet. At first the Cobbler almost fainted with shock and then he sighed deeply and said, "I haven't enough primrose leaves to make so many shoes, and besides I'd have to work right through the Summer and well into the Autumn to have them ready for you. Dear Tim, forget about your journey, besides it's far too dangerous for you to go alone. Wait until the Spring when the beetles go on their journey, by then I'll have the shoes ready and you can go with them."

Tim agreed to do as the Cobbler had suggested and later that evening he leant against his stone contentedly and dreamt of the journey he would make in the Spring.

Three Lazy Boys

There were three lazy school boys who did not feel like going to school one day. They said to one another, "Let's go and play in the woods with the animals."

First of all they met a bee and they asked the bee to come and play with them. "No, I can't," said the bee. "I have to collect pollen today for the hive."

Next, they met a fly-catcher. "Do come and play with us," they said.

"No, I'm afraid I can't play with you because I have to catch some gnats for my hungry babies."

Then they met a squirrel. "Do come and play with us, Squirrel," they said. "Sorry, I can't play today because I have to collect nuts and acorns for the Winter so that I will not be hungry when snow covers the ground," said Squirrel.

The three school boys were quite bored by this time and said to one another, "Oh well if no-one will play with us we might as well go to school." And off they went back to school.

The Lost Doll

Carl and Caroline Kangaroo were standing in the shade of a eucalyptus tree in Australia, when Carla the baby kangaroo shouted from the pouch,

"Mummy, I lost my dolly when we were jumping through the fields last night, it fell out when you did a really big jump!"

However could Mummy Kangaroo think clearly whilst Carla was crying so loudly? And what's more, where could she find another doll quickly? There was only one thing they could do and that was to jump back to the field and have a really good look for the doll.

It would soon be night time so they must hurry! They were very lucky indeed. Daddy Kangaroo saw the doll hanging from a branch of a tree, so he jumped up high enough to reach it. Carla stopped crying at once and fell asleep happily clutching the dolly in her arms. At last, Mummy and Daddy Kangaroo would get some peace!

The Wood Sprite

Once upon a time there was a jolly wood sprite who lived in the woods and who loved to play practical jokes on everyone. Every day he thought of a new trick to play.

His favourite time of year was harvest-time, blackberry picking time! Then he'd spend the whole day in search of humans — children preferably who he could play tricks on. He would pretend to help collect blackberries and then he'd be naughty and put berries in the children's hair! The children loved his funny antics.

He knew that children loved to have competitions when they picked blackberries, too. He had a lot of fun then. When he heard one of the children shouting that they had the most berries in their basket, he would pick as many as he could carry and put them in the other child's basket. Then when they looked to see who had the most — well, how did that happen — my basket was almost empty and now it's full!

The parents were always pleased when he was about because as long as he tricked the children, they kept picking more and more blackberries. Then home they would all go and Mum would make a delicious blackberry pie.

When they went mushroom picking, the wood sprite would make sure that the children never picked the poisonous ones, but at the same time he'd still get up to his pranks, and would put a snail or a worm in amongst the mushrooms, just to scare the parents! Then when everyone was arguing about who had put the snail in with the mushrooms, the wood sprite would appear and own up to the mischievous prank.

Who knows, you might meet the wood sprite when you're next in the woods. If you do meet him, be careful that he doesn't play a trick on you!

Mary and Molly

In the next few stories I am going to tell you about Mary and her kitten Molly.

One day, when Mary was 10 years old, she came running into the house, shouting, "Mummy, Mrs Jones' cat has had four really sweet kittens, can I have one, please say yes Mummy please!"

Mummy wasn't too keen to have one, but because Mary begged so much, in the end she gave in and said Mary could have one.

At once, Mary ran over to Mrs Jones' and picked up the black and white one and called her Molly. The kittens were still too young to leave their mother so Mary would have to wait a few weeks before she could take Molly home with her.

"Oh but I don't think I can wait so long," said Mary downheartedly. "Just you wait and see, the time will pass very quickly," said Mrs Jones.

The time did pass and Mary proudly took the kitten home one evening to show her mother.

A Sleepless Night

As soon as Mary brought the kitten home she gave her a saucer of milk but Molly just mewed and wouldn't drink it. "Perhaps she's not thirsty," thought Mary, "she needs to settle in first."

Mary put Molly on a cushion in a small basket, and put it in the bedroom she shared with her sister, Laura. However, there was no chance of any sleep that night because Molly mewed and mewed and kept the two girls awake.

At last Laura had an idea, "I could put my angora pullover underneath Molly then it will feel as soft as her mother and we'll be able to get some sleep at long last."

Molly lay on the angora jumper and for a short while there was silence. Then suddenly Molly began to miaow again.

"I can't stand it any longer," said Laura, "I want to sleep. Tomorrow you'd better take Molly back to Mrs Jones' because she still needs to be with her mother for a little while longer."

And that is just what Mary did.

Molly Settles In

A few weeks later Molly was old enough to leave her mother and live with Mary. She soon got used to the cat box and when Mary came home from school she would wait for Molly at the garden gate.

The two would often play together. One of Molly's favourite games was to sit on Mary's shoulder and try to knock her pencil out of her hand.

Mary made Molly a little hat and jacket, but the kitten hated them and bit and scratched them to shreds.

Mary had taken a lot of care knitting these clothes for the kitten, so she was quite upset about them being ruined.

"An animal is not a doll," said Mary's mother.

Molly's favourite toy was a ball of wool. "She's practising mousing," said Mary's mother when she saw Molly chasing the wool.

Mary found it difficult to believe that her lovely kitten could do such an awful thing. But Mary was mistaken.

Molly Disappears

One day, when Mary arrived home from school, Molly was not waiting for her by the garden gate. Mary searched everywhere for her; in the house, in the garden, under the beds, in cupboards calling, "Molly where are you?" But she was nowhere to be found.

Suddenly, Mary heard a distant miaow. She went towards where the noise was coming from, and there on the top of a high wall was Molly. The kitten had climbed up there but couldn't get down again.

Mary went to get her sister, Laura, to help carry the ladder over to the wall. They soon got Molly down and from then on Molly was known as the climbing cat!

Mary's mother explained to her that it is very natural for a cat to want to climb and explore. It is their instinct to be curious!

The Mouse-catcher

The weeks went by and Molly grew up to be a full size cat, with sharp teeth and claws.

But for Mary she was still the playful kitten, until the morning she woke up to find three dead mice on her eiderdown! "Mummy, Mummy, come quickly!" she yelled.

When Mary's mother arrived on the scene she said, "Well, well, your Molly is a real mouse-catcher! She must have climbed in through the open window and wanted to show you what she had caught." Mary now understood that Molly was a hunting animal like all cats.

Later she said to Molly, "I prefer bacon and eggs for breakfast next time, Molly, rather than mice."

Then she said, "But please don't leave anything else on my bed." Mary hoped she wasn't going to be woken up like that again! After all, what would happen if Molly caught something really big!

No Meat on Monday

It was Monday morning. Mother took some chops out of the fridge and put them on the table. Then she went to fetch the potatoes from the cupboard.

Molly meanwhile smelt the meat and slipped unnoticed into the kitchen. Mary's mother returned from the cupboard to see Molly jump down from the table, having eaten all the chops.

Mary's mother grabbed the rolling pin and chased Molly out of the kitchen.

For lunch that day there were only vegetables and potatoes, and Mary sat in silence because she felt very guilty about her kitten spoiling the family's lunch. She was in trouble again because of that naughty Molly.

The Surprise

A few weeks went by and one day Mary couldn't find Molly anywhere. Everyone shook their heads and said, "Has your cat gone climbing and got stuck again?"

Mary knew that Molly was too sensible to play tricks like that now. There must be some other reason for her sudden disappearance. She searched high and low for her but there was no sign of Molly anywhere.

As the whole family were having their evening meal they heard a loud "miaow" coming from the corner cupboard. And there they found Molly with three kittens! What a lovely surprise!

Mary, at once, wanted to hold the kittens. But her mother reminded her that she should be careful because they needed to be with their mother until they were old enough to look after themselves.

"Remember how unhappy Molly was when she was taken away from her mother too early?" said Mary's mother.

Mary had to agree and was quite happy to leave Molly to look after her babies in peace.

Mary and her sister, Laura, loved to watch the kittens playing and they gave each one a name.

Kittens for Sale

A few weeks after the kittens were born Mary's mother said, "We must decide what we are going to do with these kittens, we can't possibly keep them all."

"But Mummy, please let Molly keep one of her kittens, please." She pestered her mother for so long that in the end her mother agreed to keep one.

Mary picked out a black and grey striped one which she had called 'Maxi'. But what would they do with the others?

Mary told all the people she knew that there were two kittens for sale and she put a notice in the newsagent's window: "Kittens for sale! Mary Parkinson, No. 4 Park Avenue."

Soon the mother of a school friend came to buy one of the kittens for her daughter, and the next day a lady came to buy the other kitten which she had seen advertised in the newsagent's window.

She said, "I live on my own so a kitten will keep me company."

Mary was very happy that the kittens were going to such good homes and that she still had Molly and Maxi.

Molly and Maxi

Molly was content with Maxi the kitten that was left, and she didn't appear to miss the others.

She would play happily with Maxi, telling him off whenever he was naughty and she would never let him out of her sight.

Once, when the top was left off a milkbottle, Molly stopped Maxi from licking the cream off the top of the milk, just as Mary's mother came into the kitchen and saw them both looking rather guilty!

Every morning Molly and Maxi would try and get into Mary's bedroom. They would scratch at the door until Mary let them in.

Then they would jump into bed with Mary and her sister Laura. "This is just like having a hot water bottle," said Laura. "Except that hot water bottles don't purr," laughed Mary.

Sometimes their mother would put her head round the door and ask, "Have you seen the cats anywhere? They're not in the beds, are they?" "No, of course not," fibbed the two girls, because they knew that their mother did not allow animals in the beds.

The two girls didn't stay in bed very long once the cats had jumped in. In fact, it was a very good way to get them out of bed!

Molly's End

Molly lived happily with Mary and her family for many years and became very old.

One day she could no longer stand up, she didn't want anything to eat and wouldn't even drink her milk.

So Mary put Molly in a basket and set off on her bicycle to the vet. Mary knew the vet well and liked him very much.

He said to Mary, "It is the same with animals as it is with humans, one day their life comes to an end. Your Molly is very poorly and so the best thing to do is for me to give her an injection to put her to sleep, so that she doesn't suffer any more."

What would Mary say to this suggestion? She thought it over and a little while later she cycled home with the dead cat. When she got home she dug a hole in the garden and put her dearest Molly into it.

Then she wrote on a piece of wood, "Here lies my dearest Molly" and she placed this over the grave. She stood in tears stroking Maxi. She lifted him up and said to him, "I am glad that you are here to comfort me."

They both missed Molly for a while but Maxi kept Mary busy and amused.

Easter Joy in Austria

It was the most beautiful Easter Day that Boris could ever remember and what's more he would never forget this day.

Boris and his brother, Sebastian, had been looking forward to Easter Day for a very long time. As Boris was very young, he did not really remember any Easters from previous years. His older brother, Sebastian, had been telling him every night about Easter eggs and how delicious they are. He just couldn't wait until he was able to go searching for them, in fact he could hardly sleep that night with excitement.

Sometimes Sebastian teased Boris and told him that if he didn't behave well, there wouldn't be any eggs for him. So, Boris had tried to be very good, although it was difficult for him!

When he went looking for his Easter eggs, he found lots of brightly painted eggs in the grass and then he spotted something moving in the grass. Boris went towards it, bent down and he leapt back with amazement. "Sebastian, come quick!"

There in the grass was a tiny little wolf cub. Sebastian and the boys' parents came running to the scene to look at the little cub.

Little Boris had a new playmate and friend, at least until the wolf cub was old enough to look after himself in the wild.

In Austria it is very rare for a wild animal to seek shelter in a farm yard.

Boris was very happy with his new playmate and now all the family, Mummy, Daddy, Sebastian and Boris could enjoy Easter Day eating lots of delicious Easter eggs.

The Greedy King

There was once a King who liked to eat cherries all day long. The palace grounds were full of cherry trees, but the delicious cherries weren't only the King's favourite food but were the birds' favourite too!

This really annoyed the King and he decided that all the birds should be killed. And that is just what happened.

Soon afterwards the people in the kingdom no longer heard the birds singing in the morning. They were very sad that there were no more birds but the King was very happy because he, alone, had all the cherries!

It wasn't long, however, before there was a plague of pests — there were flies, gnats, snails, worms and beetles everywhere eating all the crops.

Soon there was a terrible famine throughout the kingdom. So the people approached the King and said, "Your Majesty, please let birds live in the kingdom again. They eat all the pests, stop the crops from being ruined, and stop us from starving."

The King realised that he had only been thinking about himself, and he sent a messenger to find birds for the kingdom. It didn't take long before the plague was over and the people had enough to eat, and the greedy King still had enough cherries to eat!

The whole of the kingdom enjoyed the sound of the birds singing in the morning again.

Mountains of Porridge

A long time ago, a poor girl and her mother lived alone in a small cottage. One day, they had nothing left to eat, the girl met a good fairy who had heard of the girl's problems. She gave the girl a present of a small pan, and told her to say the words, "Little pan, cook" and the pan would cook delicious porridge, and when she said the words "Little pan, stop cooking" the pan would stop cooking the porridge. The girl took the pan home to her mother and from then on the two were no longer hungry.

The girl went out one day and the mother said to the pan, "Little pan, cook" and the little pan cooked the porridge. The mother ate until she was full up.

Then she wanted to stop the pan cooking but she had forgotten the rhyme. So the pan cooked more and more; porridge spilled out over the cooker and soon it had filled the kitchen and the whole house. Finally, it reached the next house and then the whole street — and still it didn't stop.

At long last the girl came home and she said the magic words, "Little pan, stop cooking!" and at once, the pan stopped cooking. But now, anyone who wants to reach the town must first eat through mountains of porridge!

Mr Pepper

"What, you're stopping work so soon?" cried the birds who shared the oak tree with Mr Pepper, the squirrel. "How strange, you want to go to sleep and we're just waiting to play."

The birds were so happy that it was a nice sunny day because they had planned all sorts of games to play. One of their favourite games is to see who can collect the most worms. The youngest birds always lost because the older brothers and sisters knew where to find the worms, and there were always the biggest and fattest worms too. Anyway, off they went on their journeys, busily chattering and laughing to each other. They were still puzzled by Mr Pepper, the squirrel, though.

The squirrel did not want to be disturbed

by the birds and was satisfied with his day's work. He looked contentedly at all the hazel nuts he had collected in the early morning. Now he was well stocked up for the Winter!

He had also climbed up a pear tree and taken a pear which he had nailed on the tree. Afterwards, he had collected material for his nest.

So, Mr Pepper was not lazy, as the birds thought. He had had a busy day and he was beginning to feel sleepy now.

He closed the windows and relaxed. He dreamt of a lovely female squirrel that he had met during his busy day. Next Spring he would ask her to marry him and all the animals would be invited to the wedding. What a happy day it would be!

The Pancake Hat

Michael is watching his mother cooking. She is making pancakes. They're his favourite.

She makes the batter with flour, eggs, salt and water. Then she puts some fat into the pan and as soon as it's hot enough adds some mixture. When the pancake is golden underneath, she turns it over, so that the other side can brown. To do that, she tosses the pancake in the air and catches it in the pan. "Please may I do that too?" says Michael. "It's not as easy as it looks," warns his mother.

Michael pleads with her and finally gets his own way. He holds the pan with both hands and flings the pancake high into the air. He looks up, and there it is, stuck to the ceiling!

Just as he is looking up it comes flying down and lands smack on his head. "Now you've got a pancake hat," laughs his mother.

Michael finds it funny, too. However, he tries again and the next time when he tosses it into the air, the pancake flops straight back into the pan. He'd made his first pancake . . . at least, the first one which didn't end up on his head!

Man In The Moon

One day, long ago, a man went to the forest to cut wood. At the end of the day he had chopped a big bundle of wood, so he put it over his shoulder and set off home.

As he came to the edge of the forest he saw an old woman sitting on a log, crying. The old woman was really a fairy in disguise, and she said to the woodcutter, "Please give me a few sticks from your bundle. My fire's gone out and I'm too old to chop wood." But the woodcutter said, "Certainly not! It's taken me all day to chop this lot and I'm not giving any of it away."

Then the old woman jumped up and, throwing off her disguise, became a fairy again and said to the woodcutter, "As a punishment for your selfishness you shall be banished to the moon where you will carry your bundle of wood for ever!" If you look up at night you can still see him there.

Getting Up

"Rrr-ring — time to get up," the alarm clock shouts.

"Clean your teeth and rinse your mouth properly," says the toothbrush.

"Not so careful, I won't hurt," says the water.

"Rub hard to dry well," says the towel.

"Where does your arm go?" asks the pullover.

"We'll get your big feet in," joke the socks.

"Right leg first, then the left," the trousers command.

"At last we're on," mutter the shoes.

"We'll soon smarten you up," laugh the brush and comb.

"I'll clean your dirty nose," giggles the cheeky handkerchief.

"Ready?"

"Quite ready."

"Let's go!" they all chorus.

Bedtime

"Don't forget me," says the toothbrush.

"We'll make you clean," say the soap and facecloth.

"I'll dry you," says the fluffy, white towel.

"Put us in a neat pile," say the clothes.

"Am I packed for tomorrow?" asks the satchel.

"Please set my alarm," says the clock by the bed.

"Leave me open a little," says the window.

"Don't read too late and leave me on too long," says the bedside lamp.

"Let me into your warm bed," begs the old teddy bear.

"Sleep well and sweet dreams," says mother quietly.

"Yes, I'm coming," whispers sleep.

The Surprise Present

Pepino is a young South American boy who lives with his parents in the Andes. It is a hard life for the people in those parts.

Often their fields lie many miles away from their homes: therefore the llamas are the South Americans' favourite animal. They can carry heavy loads and go for days without food and water. Pepino's father has a strong llama who carries heavy baskets and bags for him in the fields.

One day, however, Pepino had a great surprise. His father called to him one morning from the stall, and there next to its mother was a baby llama.

"That's your very own llama," said Pepino's father. Pepino was overjoyed and thanked his father for this special gift. Pepino put his arms around the baby and whispered, "I am Pepino and your name is Pedro."

Pepino would remember this day for ever, as the happiest day of his life.

Pedro's First Journey

Pepino's llama, Pedro, soon grew up to be a strong, healthy animal. One day Pepino's father decided it was time to harvest the potatoes.

However, the potato field was so far away that it would take a whole day to get there. So he packed up his llama with baskets and a blanket. Pepino asked, "Could Pedro and I come with you? Pedro is very big now and perhaps he could help with the carrying."

Pepino's father replied, "His legs are still far too thin and his back is still too weak to carry anything, but he can come along all the same."

Pepino ran into the house to get his things for the journey. He went up to Pedro with his bundle and said, "Dad thinks that you are too weak to help with the carrying, but you will be able to carry my small bundle. Besides, you must get used to carrying things on your back whenever you go out."

Pedro didn't mind the bundle on his back and set off quite happily with Pepino on his first journey. Pepino's father chuckled to himself and was very glad to see his son getting on so well with the llama.

Pepino chatted to his father and to Pedro. He enjoyed being with his father and learned many things from him about looking after animals and about farming. Pepino's father was glad to have someone to talk to.

Harvest-Time

Father and son travelled together with the two llamas for several hours. Whenever Pepino grew tired he was allowed to ride on Pedro's back for a short while.

At nightfall, Pepino's father laid out the blanket and the two slept in the open air, beneath the stars. The next morning, they set off again until they reached the potato field.

Then the big llama had to tow a type of plough through the field so that the soil would be dug and would free the potatoes that were buried under the ground. Pepino went behind his father and put the potatoes into sacks and baskets, until his back ached from bending down so much.

Meanwhile Pedro stood at the edge of the field and grazed. The work was soon completed, since Pepino's father only harvested as many potatoes as the llama could carry. He lit a small camp fire and let Pepino cook a few potatoes on it. Nothing had ever tasted as good!

Then when Pepino's father had loaded up his llama, he insisted that Pedro was strong enough to carry some of the potatoes. So Pedro carried one basket and they all set off for home.

This time, of course, Pepino couldn't ride on Pedro's back when he was tired! They arrived home safe and sound, and Pepino was exhausted but very proud because he had helped, just like a grown-up. His mother, too, was very pleased with her young son. He was turning into a fine young man.

Shearing!

One day Pepino's father said to him, "Today, we're going to shear Pedro because his coat is too thick." Of course, Pepino knew that llamas are shorn just as sheep are and their wool is used to make warm blankets, but he was still horrified at the thought of his llama being shorn.

Pepino thought shorn llamas looked extremely ugly. So he tried to change his father's mind, but had no luck. "Look, Pepino," he said, "it will grow again and Pedro will have a thick coat just as before. You know that we need the wool, so be sensible." With that he fetched the shears and began to shear Pedro. Pepino watched him and made a face at his father as he sheared.

When he had finished, a mound of wool lay on the floor and Pedro looked so thin! Pepino put his arm around him and said, "Just you wait and see, Pedro, you'll soon have your woolly coat again."

"Yes, and then I'll get my shears out again," said Pepino's father, laughing. "Come to think of it, young man, it's time you had a hair cut too!"

Pepino goes to School

A few months went by. Then one day Pepino's father said, "Pepino, it is time that you went to school and learnt something of the world outside this village. You must learn to read and write."

As the school is a long way from Pepino's home, Pedro must take him and now that Pedro is fully-grown, Pepino can ride on his back. Pepino's mother gave him a sandwich and some sweets to take to school.

When they arrived at school, Pedro wanted to ride into the classroom. "That's not allowed," said the teacher. "Your llama can't come into the class, he must wait outside." Pepino was very disappointed, but there was nothing he could do about it. He tied Pedro up outside the school and said to him, "I won't be long. You can eat the grass while you wait for me."

Pepino sat down in the classroom and the lesson began. Later, when the teacher was writing the first few letters of the alphabet on the blackboard Pedro stuck his head through the open window. He looked curiously around the classroom. Everyone roared with laughter and the teacher said, "That's the very first llama ever to have lessons from me! If you stay quite still, you can look on today but you must stay outside from tomorrow onwards."

Pepino's Plan

Pepino rides daily to and from school on Pedro. He enjoys school very much, especially when the teacher tells stories of distant countries, and of foreign peoples and their work, as well as unheard-of machines and of motor cars, aeroplanes and trains.

But most of all Pepino is fascinated by a thing called electricity. Whenever he sees his mother with the oil lamp he thinks, "If only she had this wonderful thing known as electricity! She would be able to press a switch and the whole room would light up — that must be a fantastic sight!"

So Pepino decided to earn enough money to be able to buy his mother some electricity. He approached Antonio, a shopkeeper, and asked, "Have you any work that Pedro and I could do for you?" Antonio had plenty for them to do. So, each evening after school, Pepino and Pedro would go and work for Antonio, carrying boxes and sacks for the customers.

Pepino saved up the money he had earned for this work, until one day he decided he must have enough money to go to town and buy some electricity for his mother. "What a surprise that will be for Mummy," he thought as he fell asleep that night, and he was very excited about buying this special present!

Disappointment!

The next day Pepino and Pedro set out for the town that Pepino had heard the teacher mention in the lessons. They set off happily and made good progress as the path was not too bumpy or stony.

But as night fell they still had not reached the town. "It must be further than we thought," Pepino remarked to Pedro. "We'd better find a sheltered spot to spend the night." Pepino got down from Pedro, led him by the reins and they began to look for a nice spot in which to spend the night.

Suddenly Pepino heard a noise, and saw a man sitting on a mule. "Hello, little one, where are you going? Have you lost your way?" the man asked Pepino. "No," said Pepino sharply, "I'm riding to town to buy some electricity." Hearing this the man burst out laughing and laughed until he went blue in the face.

"That's the funniest thing I've heard in years," he said. "You can't buy electricity just like that, first you have to build a power station, everybody knows that. I think you ought to go home, your parents must be really worried about you by now."

Pepino was bitterly disappointed. Sadly, he and Pedro set off back home. On the way, Pepino made up his mind to ask the teacher whether what the man said about the power station was correct. Perhaps he could build one when he's older and wiser!

Crafty Pedro

One evening Pepino's father said, "I was offered a really good price for Pedro today. I think it would be a good idea to sell him!" Pepino went white with shock as he heard his father say this. "But, Daddy, you can't sell my best friend!"

"Listen Pepino, our other llama, Pedro's mother, is going to have another baby soon and you can have the baby llama to look after yourself. You know how much I need the money," said Pepino's father. Pepino went to Pedro's stall and he said to him with tears in his eyes, "Pedro, you're to be sold. We've got to try and stop this somehow or other. If only I could think of a way."

The next day, the prospective buyer came to have a look at Pedro. Firstly, he walked round Pedro and said, "He's not a bad looking llama." Then when he held on to Pedro to test his coat, Pedro spat in the man's face. The man was furious and stepped away from the llama. When he dared to go near Pedro again, the llama kicked the man with one of his hind legs. "Ouch, that hurt. What an unfriendly animal that llama is," said the man.

Pepino's father scratched his head in disbelief and insisted that Pedro was a kind, gentle llama really and that he couldn't understand why he was behaving so badly. "Well I don't want to buy him now," said the man, "he's untameable." Pepino stroked his friend's head and said happily, "Well done, Pedro, that did the trick."

Llama Breeding

Pepino's father now realised that it would break his son's heart if he were to sell Pedro. "Father," said Pepino, "if we sell Pedro's wool that will give you some money, and when the baby llama grows up we'll be able to sell that wool too."

Pepino's father laughed, "I can see that you're turning into a real llama breeder and I thought you said you wanted to build a power station!" "Oh, I can do that later!" replied Pepino, "but first I must see to the llamas."

"We need a new stall that's bigger than the old one," added Pepino later that day. "From the money we get for the wool we can buy another llama, a female one would be best."

Pepino continued to make plans until he went to bed that evening, completely exhausted. "I'm going to be a famous llama breeder," he mused as he fell into a deep, dreamy sleep, happy that he was going to be able to keep his beloved Pedro.

The Racoons go Fishing

High up in the mountains in North America live a family of racoons. They are happy creatures with long, bushy tails. The young ones are especially fun loving and play all day long in the branches of the trees.

When they were fully grown, Father Racoon said to his children, "Now you're old enough to learn how to fish. Follow me." They climbed down the tree and walked until they reached the bank of a mountain lake. The young ones just stared in amazement at the water as they had never left their home in the tree before.

"Now we shall fish," said Father Racoon. He dipped his front paw into the water and beat it about until he caught a silver coloured fish that swam up to him. "That's how it's done," he said, "just do what I did and you'll soon be real fishermen."

No sooner said than done. The young racoons loved fishing even more than playing in the trees! It was not long before the young racoons became very good fishermen and could catch at least ten fish a day!

The Snowdrop

It was still Winter. Deep in the earth, the snowdrop was sleeping, in its bulb. One day, rain fell and the raindrops broke through the snow-covered ground and reached the sleeping snowdrop.

The raindrops told the snowdrop bulb of the bright, light world above the ground. Soon after the rain, the sun shone and the rays of sunshine penetrated beneath the snow until it, too, reached the sleeping bulb.

"Do help me," said the bulb. "I'm not yet strong enough to push through the earth, and yet I feel that if I stretch out enough I shall be able to break through the surface and reach the daylight." With the help of the sun, the snowdrop bulb stretched and pushed until she finally emerged from the soil.

The snow was bitterly cold but the early Spring sunshine warmed her a little, and she raised her little head courageously as she heard the people passing by say, "Look over there, the first snowdrop. At last, Spring's on its way!" This cheered the snowdrop greatly even though it was still freezing cold.

Talking Shoes

The town clock struck midnight — soon the shoe shop would come to life. The shoes jumped down from the shelves and began to chatter amongst themselves.

"You can say what you like," said the elegant ladies' shoes, "but we are the best of all." And they twirled, so that all the other shoes could see their fine leather and their dainty heels.

"Look at us," called the children's shoes, "we're better than the ladies' shoes because we're more colourful." And then they hopped and jumped round the room. "Poppycock!" retorted the gentlemen's boots. "We are by far the best of all because we are so solid and strong." And they marched up and down in step.

"Oh no, you're not the best," said the pair of slippers. "We are, because we are soft and comfortable." And they crept quietly around the room. "You've all forgotten about us!" cried the pair of wellingtons. "We're smooth and shiny, of course we are the best."

The shoes would have carried on this argument for hours if the clock had not struck one. At that moment they all leapt back on to the shelves.

What a pity that they could not ask little Thomas which were the best, because he would have said bare feet! Because he never wears shoes!

The Stubborn Turnip

Daddy has grown some turnips. One day he goes to pull one up. He seizes the top and pulls and pulls, but it won't come up. Daddy calls Mummy to help. Mummy pulls Daddy, Daddy pulls the turnip. They pull and pull, but they can't get it to come out.

Little George arrives. Little George pulls Mummy, Mummy pulls Daddy, Daddy pulls the turnip. They pull and pull, but they still can't get it out.

The dog comes along. The dog pulls Little George, Little George pulls Mummy, Mummy pulls Daddy, Daddy pulls the turnip. They pull and pull, but they still can't get it out.

The chicken comes along. The chicken pulls the dog, the dog pulls Little George, Little George pulls Mummy, Mummy pulls Daddy, Daddy pulls the turnip. They pull and pull but they still can't get it out.

The cock comes along. The cock pulls the chicken, the chicken pulls the dog, the dog pulls Little George, Little George pulls Mummy, Mummy pulls Daddy, Daddy pulls the turnip. They pull and pull, until — Hooray! At last the turnip's out and the story is over.

The Vanishing Rabbit

Suzanne was given a snow-white rabbit for her seventh birthday. She called him Cuddles, because of his cuddly white fur, and loved him dearly. She fed him lettuce and dandelions, brushed his coat every day, and talked to him for hours.

Yesterday, she put her rabbit into her old doll's pram and took him for a walk in the garden. She talked to Cuddles all the time, telling him the names of the flowers. She showed him where the dandelion leaves were growing for they were his favourite. She also told him to stay away from Daddy's vegetable patch! He would be in a lot of trouble if he started to nibble at the young carrots and cabbages. When it started to rain, she brought the pram into the living room. She went into the kitchen for a second to get Cuddles some food, but when she returned he had disappeared!

He must have jumped out of the pram. Suzanne searched the whole room; under the table, behind the armchairs, in the knitting basket and even under the carpet! She lay flat on the floor to look under the cupboards — but there was no sign of Cuddles. "Cuddles, little rabbit, come out, where are you hiding?" she pleaded, but with no luck. Poor Suzanne was nearly in tears, so her mother came to help her search. Cuddles was nowhere to be found. That evening, Suzanne went sadly to bed — she missed her rabbit terribly.

Imagine her joy when she came into the living room in the morning and found her rabbit sitting quietly on the carpet.

"Cuddles, dear Cuddles, where on earth have you been?" she cried, and hugged the rabbit.

The Puzzled Gnome

Once upon a time there was a woodcutter, who was working deep in the forest on a cold Winter's day. A friendly gnome appeared to watch him work. The gnome hopped about, trying to keep out of the woodcutter's way. Every now and then the woodcutter put his axe down and blew on his cold hands. "Why are you doing that?" asked the gnome. "I'm warming my hands," answered the woodcutter.

At lunch time he made a fire from some of the smaller sticks and put a pot of soup on it. When he came to drink the soup it had got too hot. So he blew on it.

The gnome asked him, "Are you blowing on the soup because it isn't hot enough?"

"No," answered the woodcutter, "I'm blowing on it to cool it down."

The gnome was puzzled and shook his head in wonder. "You're certainly a strange creature," he said. "You can blow both hot and cold air. I'm not going to stay with you." Saying this he stood up and vanished.

A Place for the Greedy

The land of milk and honey lies three miles behind Christmas. To get there, you turn right, left and then follow your nose. If you want to get in, you must first eat your way through a sweet pudding mountain.

When you get there you'll find that the houses are roofed with pancakes, the doors made of marzipan, the windows of icing and the walls of bacon. All the fences are made of sausages and the streets are paved with cheese.

The springs gush with best orange juice and the streams flow with wonderful wine. The trees in the forest bear biscuits, nuts and sweets, whilst the bushes are hung with freshly baked rolls. No-one in the land of milk and honey ever goes hungry. They just lie on their backs and open their mouths. Roast chicken and ducks fly overhead. Roast pigs roam the fields and when it rains, it rains honey. The snow is ice-cream, the hail is boiled sweets, nuts, raisins and figs.

The land of milk and honey is a fine country, but only for the lazy and greedy. Work is strictly forbidden and the King is the fattest and most stupid of all.

There must be much better places to visit than this one full of lazy and greedy people! Aren't you glad you don't live there?

Saint Martin

Late one Winter's evening Saint Martin was riding through the woods. The ground was frozen and it was snowing hard. Martin pulled his coat tightly round his body to protect himself from the icy cold.

Then, he suddenly saw an old beggar sitting at the edge of the path wearing only a short jacket and obviously freezing cold. Saint Martin stopped his horse and said to the man, "Good fellow, how can I help you? I have no gold or silver and my sword is surely of no use to you."

Then he stopped in the middle of his speech and cut his huge, warm coat into two pieces and gave one half to the beggar and kept the other for himself. After wrapping the old beggar in his half of the coat he rode into the darkness and disappeared.

In the middle of the night, Saint Martin dreamt he saw the old beggar wearing half his coat and saying, "You're very kind-hearted, Saint Martin, and you will therefore be rewarded in heaven."

Green Steven

There was once a little boy called Steven, and morning, noon and night he ate nothing but green jelly. Even when his mother cooked other delicious dishes such as chicken, cakes and biscuits Steven refused to eat them.

Instead, he insisted on eating yet more green jelly. Steven's mother shook her head and heaved a great sigh and said, "If only green jelly were good for you!"

One day when Steven went into the bathroom, his mother dropped her toothbrush in disbelief. She yelled, "Just look at yourself." Steven looked at himself in the mirror and could not believe his eyes — he was green from top to toe!

"Go straight to bed this minute," said his mother. "You can't possibly go to school, looking like that. I'll call the doctor."

When the doctor arrived, he examined Steven and said, "He's been eating too much green jelly. In future, he must eat other foods such as tomatoes, eggs, fish, meat, milk and potatoes."

A week later Steven's colour had returned to normal. From now on he did not dare to eat as much green jelly as he used to.

Now he eats all the things his mother cooks for him and if he sees any of his friends eating too much green jelly, he tells them what happened to him when he only ate green jelly!

You would not want that to happen to you, would you? It is best to eat a little of everything, then you will be strong and healthy.

Roland and the Pepper

When Roland was seven years old, he went on holiday to Greece with his parents. They stayed in Poros in a villa by the sea. It was the first time that Roland had been abroad on holiday and he found Greece fascinating.

Just round the corner, was a shop where you could buy groceries, wine, toothpaste, and newspapers. Roland enjoyed watching the shopkeeper serve the customers especially when he had to weigh aubergines or peppers or cut a wedge of cheese and when he poured olive oil into bottles.

One day a lady came in and asked for 'Piperi'. Roland had no idea what 'Piperi' might be, but when he saw the shopkeeper weigh out some black peppercorns he knew what the customer wanted.

Roland's nose was at the same level as the scales and he suddenly sneezed, "Atischoo" and again he sneezed and all the black peppercorns were blown all round the shop! The shopkeeper weighed out more peppercorns and this time Roland held his nose so that he did not sneeze and blow the peppercorns all over the room again!

Roland Buys a Loaf

When Roland had been in Greece several weeks and had learnt to speak a little Greek, he asked his mother if he could go alone to the baker's to buy a loaf of bread. There was only one sort of bread and it cost 12 drachma.

So Roland's mother gave him the right money and told him to say, "Ena psomi, parakalo," and then the baker would give him a loaf of bread.

Roland repeated this phrase to himself as he walked to the shop. When he said the phrase to the shopkeeper, the baker roared with laughter and said, "Let's speak English! I lived in England for several years when I was a young man."

Roland was very disappointed because he had really wanted to try out his Greek on the baker! I wonder what Roland had said to make the baker laugh so much.

Arabian

In a small Greek village lived the farmer Stefano. He had a donkey that was not grey like other donkeys, but was such a dark colour that he resembled an Arab stallion, hence his name — Arabian.

Each day Arabian carried heavy loads of almonds, grapes and straw in baskets strapped on his back for his master. Arabian was a very placid animal and took everything in his stride.

All was well until they took the donkey on holiday to the seaside. On the beach there were lots of children who were thrilled at the sight of Arabian. They were allowed to ride the donkey, and he enjoyed taking the children for rides as they were a lot lighter than the loads he normally had to carry.

When the holidays were over Arabian had to go back to work and carry heavy baskets again for his master. However, he bucked and became very stubborn when the baskets were put on his back. He did not like being back at work after the holidays.

Arabian wished that it was Summer again and he could take the little children for rides because they were so much lighter than the heavy baskets! "If only it could be the holidays all the time!" thought Arabian to himself.

The Way to the Beach

One day Roland and his parents drove along the coast in search of a fine sandy beach. They soon found one and decided to spend the day there.

They parked the car at the edge of the road and went by foot along the narrow path that led to the beach, through a vineyard. They saw a farmer's wife busy laying out the grapes to dry in the sun so that they would then become raisins.

"Kalimera!" called Roland to the lady (which means 'Hello' in English). "Kalimera!" called the lady in reply as she came towards him. She pointed to Roland that he should open his beach bag and then she filled it with delicious grapes. The whole family thanked the lady for this gift and set off for the beach again.

As they went on their way, they were given figs, tomatoes, almonds and more grapes by other farmers. Roland and his family were so happy to be on holiday in Greece and the Greek people were so very generous and friendly to them.

The Chestnut Tree

The vain chestnut tree was very happy because it could keep all its leaves. Winter came and the first snow flakes fell. The chestnut tree was delighted at the sight of the snow flakes and thought it looked even more beautiful than ever laden with snow on its branches.

It snowed more and more until snow completely covered all the leaves and branches of the chestnut tree and it was weighed down by the heavy snow. The other trees did not suffer in this way, because the snow dropped off their branches, as they had no leaves where the snow could collect.

The branches of the chestnut tree began to break off with the weight of the snow. "Help!" cried the chestnut tree. "I'm losing all my branches."

The sun heard the little tree's cries and because it felt sorry for the young tree it melted the snow with its warm rays. Then the wind returned and said to the vain chestnut tree, "I did warn you, but you wouldn't listen to my advice." The chestnut tree begged the wind to remove its leaves and said it was sorry about being so vain and stupid. The little chestnut tree had learnt its lesson.

Once upon a time there was a young chestnut tree which considered itself to be the finest tree in the whole park. In Spring it had the most beautiful white blossom, in Summer the loveliest leafy canopy and in Autumn the most colourful leaves and the shiniest chestnuts. The young chestnut tree thought so anyway.

Only one thing made it unhappy and that was when the Winter wind blew off all its leaves and left the tree completely bare. The chestnut tree had to stay like that, all bare and ugly until the following Spring.

As it was now Autumn once again the wind began to blow all the leaves from the trees. The little chestnut tree called out to the wind, "Stop blowing so hard, I want to keep my lovely leaves! I want to be as beautiful in Winter as I am now!"

The wind shook his head and tried to persuade the little tree against this idea. But the little tree pleaded so much that in the end the wind gave in. "You'll regret this decision," murmured the wind as it went on its way.

39

The Birthday Present

Robert collected all his savings together and decided to go shopping to buy his mother a birthday present. He wandered around the town for a while looking at all the different displays in the shop windows but could not find anything he liked.

Then he stopped by an automatic photograph machine and he watched people having themselves photographed. They sat on a small stool, adjusted to suit their height. Then they put money in the slot, looked into the mirror and pressed a red button. There were some flashes and after four minutes the photos slid out of the machine. Robert was fascinated.

"That would make a really good present for Mummy," Robert thought — a picture of him that she could keep in her purse to show to all her friends. Just then a tall man left the photo booth and it was Robert's turn.

He sat down, put in the right amount of money, pressed the red button and looked straight ahead. He kept quite still when the flashes went off.

Then he waited excitedly for the photos. Imagine how disappointed he was when he saw the pictures. All that could be seen of his face was a mop of golden hair! Robert could not understand it, he'd done all the things he was supposed to do, or had he?

Paul, the Astronaut

Paul wants to be an astronaut. He has read lots of books on the subject and has watched lots of television programmes about the moon and the planets.

One day, in the middle of a boring Mathematics lesson he started daydreaming about how exciting it would be to travel through the sky as an astronaut. He would be able to fly into school, without having to take care crossing the road; he would be able to watch football games without having to pay for a ticket; he would be able to visit the doves on the roof; he would be able to . . .

"Paul, your turn now, what is the answer to this problem?" asked the teacher. Oh dear! The teacher was asking him a question and he had no idea of the answer, because he had been daydreaming. "I think Paul is in cloud-cuckoo land today!" said the teacher to the rest of the class. "If the teacher only knew how right he was!" thought Paul to himself.

The Football

The football game was well under way. The ball went all over the place. It was kicked, pushed, thrown and stepped on until it felt quite dizzy!

"I can't stand it any more," shouted the football at the top of his voice. "This is no life for me, I'm off."

So, when a player kicked the ball especially high, the football decided to go on a journey by himself. He went whizzing over towns and villages and thoroughly enjoyed himself.

However, as night fell he began to feel tired so he landed in the middle of a forest. He soon found a nice place to sleep.

Early next morning he was surrounded by a group of monkeys. "What is it?" cried the monkeys excitedly. One after another the monkeys inspected the football. After trying first of all to eat the football and then to climb on it, one clever young monkey decided to kick the ball to his friend, and soon a game of football had begun.

"If only I'd known this would happen, I'd have stayed at home after all," said the football wistfully.

The Bewitched Dog

Every evening when Susan went to bed she heard Patch, the next-door neighbour's dog barking. Susan was very fond of Patch but felt sorry for him because he was always chained up in his kennel and very rarely let out.

"Why does he always bark so much?" wondered Susan. "Perhaps he's trying to tell me something," she thought as she fell asleep one night.

Susan dreamt that Patch stood by her bed and said to her, "I am really a bewitched prince and only you can help to free me." "How?" asked Susan. "You must unchain me from the kennel and then I shall be free," replied Patch. As soon as he had said this, he vanished.

When daylight broke, Susan woke up and leapt out of bed at once. She wanted to tell the neighbours about the dream and to persuade them to let Patch out of his kennel more often.

The Oak Tree

At the edge of the wood stood a mighty old oak tree. It had strong branches and its trunk was so wide that lots of animals could make their homes in the old tree.

At the top, lived a pair of bluetits, a little lower down the tree lived the squirrel in his nest, and beneath him lived the woodpecker. A wise old owl also lived in the oak and a family of mice lived amongst the tree's roots.

For many years, the animals had led quiet contented lives in the tree. Sometimes, a deer or a hare would visit them, or perhaps a swallow would rest on the branches as it flew past. This pleasant way of life could have carried on for years if something very unpleasant had not happened!

One day a lorry drove into the wood and dumped saws and axes and a lot of workmen. They walked round the oak tree and then one of them began to hack away at the oak tree with an axe.

The animals knew what was happening — their home was being chopped down! The owl flew round the tree, crying, "Run for safety everyone at once!" All the animals ran for cover away from the tree. A little later, the workmen began to use the electric saw to cut down the tree, and the animals looked on from a sheltered spot as the tree fell to the ground with an almighty thump.

"Our lovely home!" sighed the animals. "Where are we going to live now? What a pity that the humans didn't think of us when they decided to chop down the oak tree," said the animals to each other.

Disobedience!

At the edge of a large corn field lived a family of hares with their many children. "Stay close to your mother and me, children, because you're too young to go wandering off on your own since you know nothing of the dangers of the world," said Daddy Hare to the little ones. The baby hares all promised to do as their father said.

One day, however, Hoppy, the youngest and most curious baby hare, decided to go and investigate what was in the middle of the corn field. It was Autumn and the corn was just ready for harvesting. Hoppy jumped through the corn nibbling it as he went and he even stopped to chat to a field mouse on his way to the middle of the field.

Then, suddenly he heard a loud noise which was coming nearer and nearer and growing louder and louder all the time. Petrified, Hoppy looked towards the noise and saw that rolling up to him was a huge machine made of steel and with whirring bits attached to it that were sucking in the corn as it went through the field. "I must get out of the way," thought Hoppy to himself and quickly he jumped out of the way and set off for home as fast as he could.

He arrived home puffing and panting and gabbled the story of his adventure to his parents. "You saw a shredder," said his father. "It takes in the corn and throws out the stalks afterwards. You had a very narrow escape indeed!" "Hoppy, you must never go off on your own again without telling me first," said his mother sternly. And Hoppy promised that he would obey his mother's wishes from then on.

The Greedy Giant

Once upon a time, there was a very greedy giant who loved to eat and drink all day long. Every day he would eat two loaves of bread, three pints of milk, a pound of sausages and three chickens, and he would still feel hungry!

His wife pleaded with him not to eat so much. "Don't eat so much, you're going to get so fat that one day you won't be able to fit through the doorway!" But the giant took no notice of what his wife said and carried on eating as much as he wanted.

One day, he was walking through a cornfield when his tummy began to rumble with hunger. The giant reached out and grabbed a handful of corn and swallowed it greedily. Too late! He hadn't noticed that he had swallowed a field mouse that was hiding in the corn!

The giant hopped from one foot to the other, and his tummy ached as the mouse began to run around inside his stomach. He rushed off towards the Doctor's but the Doctor wasn't very sympathetic towards him. "This is a result of being so greedy," said the doctor sharply. "I can't do anything to help you, I'm afraid, all I can do is offer you some advice — go and eat a cat and then hope that the cat will catch the mouse!"

So the giant went thoughtfully home — whether he acted on the doctor's advice, no one knows.

Emile, The Giraffe

Emile, the giraffe, lived in the zoo. He had plenty to eat, but it was so boring being stared at all day long that Emile decided to go and look for a job.

He went into the town and searched for work. But everyone he approached said that they had no work for him because his long legs and neck would only get in the way all the time.

Emile was walking sadly around the town when he saw a group of people standing outside a house. They were all talking excitedly to each other and were looking upwards. Emile looked up and saw a little girl sitting on the balcony, crying because she could not get down. Emile stood close to the balcony and said to the little girl, "Hold on tight to my neck and then slide down it." The little girl did this and landed safely on the ground. Everyone cheered, "Hurrah, well done, Emile!"

In the meantime the fire brigade had arrived on the scene and the chief fireman went up to Emile and said, "You'd make a great fireman, would you like to be one?" Emile agreed at once and became the first ever giraffe to be in the fire brigade.

From then on, Emile was never bored again and in his spare time he would go to the children's playground and let the children slide down his neck!

The Sparrow Catcher

Once, there was a farmer's boy called Michael. He got on well with all kinds of animals, but especially with the birds.

One day he caught three sparrows which he decided to take home with him. As he had no bag or sack with him, he put the birds under his hat so that they would not escape.

On the way home, he met the mayor. Michael wanted to walk past the mayor without greeting him, but the mayor called out to Michael, "Aren't you going to greet your friendly mayor then?" "Good day, sir!" called Michael raising his hat a little. Wheeee! The sparrows flew out from under the hat and hit the startled mayor in the face! From then on Michael was known as the Sparrow Catcher.

The Car Wash

There was once a brand new little red car whose owner was very proud of his new purchase. One day the owner said, "It's time for you to be washed." I don't mind, thought the little car to itself, as it dreamed of soapy water and the gentle hands that would clean it.

They set off through the town to the garage. On the way, they saw the postman delivering letters. The owner of the car stopped to ask the postman if he had anything for him. "No letters today, but that's a very nice little red car," said the postman. "Thank you," said the owner, "I'm just taking it to the car wash."

Suddenly, a very loud noise came up behind them — it was a large bus. All the passengers looked and smiled at the little red car because it had had quite a shock and looked a bit frightened. The little car soon calmed down and its owner felt very proud driving round the town.

Then the owner drove the little red car to a large garage and it was petrified at the sight of so many large brushes and hoses. The noise, too, was tremendous. As the little car thought how awful this place was, a spray of water spurted towards it and the brushes started to whirl round and to scrub it, and there were soon suds everywhere, so many in fact that the little red car couldn't see anything. Then a warm wind blew from all sides and soon dried the car and it could see again.

It wasn't so bad after all, thought the little red car to itself later on. It just takes a bit of getting used to, that's all!

Ann Gives Herself Away

"It's way past your bedtime, go up to bed now, please," said Ann's mother for the fifth time. "Oh, but Mum there's a really good film on television tonight, please can I stay up to watch it?" pleaded Ann. "No, you've got school tomorrow and besides it's not a film for children."

Ann complained bitterly that her brother was allowed to stay up. "Don't forget, Ann, he is older than you. When he was your age he had to go to bed when I told him to."

Ann begged and begged to be allowed to stay up but her mother did not give in. So in the end Ann reluctantly went to bed.

Later on, when her parents and brother were all watching the film, Ann crept down the stairs and slipped, unnoticed, into the lounge. She crouched down behind an old arm chair and could just see the television from where she was hiding. The film was really exciting with lots of chases and fights. Then some dust got into Ann's nose and made her sneeze — "Atischoooo".

Everyone jumped up to see who had made the noise and her mother called out, "Who was that?" She soon found Ann, looking very guilty behind the chair. They all had to laugh, because Ann had given herself away!

Ann was so relieved that her parents had thought it was funny, that she went straight up to bed and stayed there.

A Good Idea

John and David are cousins and great friends as well. On the day before Mother's Day they were playing together in the garden at their Grandma's house. They climbed trees and made a den in the holly bush.

Suddenly John had an idea. "David, have you bought a present for Mother's Day yet?" David had learnt a poem at school which he was going to recite to his mother because he had not enough pocket money to buy a present. "Let's pick a bunch of flowers for our mothers," said John. "There's loads of flowers here in Grandma's garden."

Then David had an even better idea. They asked their Grandma first, then the two boys set to work at once gathering flowers.

A little later the two boys set up a table at the garden gate. They arranged the flowers into neat bunches, and put them into jam jars with water to keep the flowers fresh. Whenever anyone went past, they would call out, "Show your mother you care. Buy a lovely bunch of flowers for Mother's Day, only 25p a bunch." Naturally, all the passers-by stopped and bought the bunches of flowers.

Soon all the flowers were sold and John and David counted up how much money they had collected — they had more than £2 each! So they hurried to the shops to buy a nice present for their own mothers for Mother's Day.

The Last Dumpling

Once there were two young men called Fritz and Heinz who were sitting in a restaurant feeling very bored. Suddenly Fritz said, "I bet you, I can eat twenty dumplings one after the other."

Heinz couldn't believe what he had heard, but he agreed to the bet and said, "If you eat twenty dumplings then you can have the feather on my hat." "Agreed," replied Fritz and he then ordered twenty dumplings.

Fritz ate the first one very quickly and then he got slower and slower, the more dumplings he ate. After twelve dumplings he had to have a little rest, and then he ate another five. He ate the eighteenth one with great difficulty and he felt very full-up and very ill indeed as he ate the nineteenth.

One last dumpling lay on the plate, but Fritz just could not face eating it and he said, "If I'd known I wouldn't be able to eat this dumpling then I'd have eaten it first!" Heinz laughed at this and was pleased that he could keep his feather.

What did they mean? Would Fritz really have won the bet if he'd eaten the last dumpling first?

The Slice of Bread

In the middle of the school yard there lay a half-eaten slice of bread that a child had thoughtlessly thrown away. What a nasty thing to do, thought the slice of bread to itself. So at midnight it jumped up and ran through the streets to the baker's shop.

It slipped in through an open window and went into the back room where all the loaves and rolls which had been baked that night were waiting to be put in the shop window the next morning.

"Don't let yourselves be sold," said the slice of bread, "look what happened to me — half eaten by some school child and then just thrown away." When the loaves and rolls heard this they all decided to run away from the baker's with the slice of bread.

The next day there was no bread in the town, nor the day after. The people of the town were very puzzled and missed the bread very much. They all realized how much they had taken the bread for granted in the past.

A week later the loaves returned and no-one ever threw away a slice of bread again. They even used the scraps up for toast or they made bread and butter pudding. The mothers told their children to eat up all their sandwiches and not to waste any bread, otherwise they would have to go without their lunch again!

Lucy, the Baby Mouse

Lucy was the youngest of five baby mice and the merriest and cheekiest.

One day she decided she would like to go alone to visit her poor relation, Polly the church mouse, who lived more than one hundred mouse miles away.

This poor little church mouse had so little to eat that she would sometimes have to nibble the cushions on the church pews.

On one occasion Polly had even gnawed at the bell rope and the next Sunday, when the bell ringer tried to ring the bell to call everyone to church, it was silent! Since then, Polly lived at the very back of the church because she was frightened of being caught.

Lucy had always liked Polly because she made her laugh. Although Polly was older than Lucy, they used to play together all day and have such fun. Then Polly's family had to move away and Lucy missed her so much. It also made her sad to think of Polly being hungry and she wanted to take Polly a large basket of food.

Lucy begged her mother to let her go to visit Polly. Her mother was not happy about it, because Lucy had not travelled so far by herself before. Lucy's mother finally gave in and let her go to visit Polly and she packed up a parcel of cheese, corn and some bacon rind for Lucy to give to Polly.

Polly was thrilled at seeing Lucy and very grateful for the food. The two mice chattered together for hours and then before nightfall Lucy set off home feeling very pleased that she had been able to persuade her mother to let her go to Polly's on her own.

Lucy went to bed thinking about all the things she and Polly had been talking about. She could not wait to see her cousin again and was planning her next visit already.

The Swallow's Nest

Last Spring a pair of swallows built a nest in our roof. They brought up many children there and we were able to watch them learn to fly. In the Autumn when it got cooler, the whole family flew off to the other side of the world to spend the Winter in a hotter place.

When they left, the nest was empty and we did not have anything to watch, but not for long. Soon a pair of sparrows moved into the swallows' nest because they were too lazy to build their own, and they stayed there all through the Winter.

We wondered what would happen when the swallows returned in the Spring to reclaim their old nest. Then one day we heard lots of noises coming from the nest and suddenly the whole thing fell to the ground. The nest was broken but the sparrows were unharmed. They flew off and found another nest to live in.

When the swallows returned in the Spring, they began to build a new nest in our roof, so there is still a swallows' nest under our roof and Mrs Swallow watches over the babies every Spring. We are really happy about this because it is said that swallows bring good luck.

The Washing Line

One day when the sun was very hot indeed the flowers in the flower bed were wilting and gasping for a drink.

How could the poor flowers possibly get a drink; everyone had forgotten all about them.

Oh! good, here comes some-one. But there was no sign of a watering can or a hose — just a basket full of wet washing.

As the washing was being pegged out on the line, the flowers could feel spots of water! What's this, they thought — and then, more and more drops of water, until the washing line was full of wet washing and it was dripping all over the flower bed and watering it!

The Pelican Crossing

May I introduce myself? I am a pelican crossing and I stand at a very important cross roads.

In the early morning, when all the grown-ups drive to work and the children go to school, I'm kept very busy indeed! I get used to most things, but really I must tell you about what happened yesterday.

I was showing 'green' for the cars, that means showing 'red' for pedestrians. Unfortunately, however, there are always pedestrians who do not pay attention to the little green man. Yesterday, there was a pedestrian in a hurry so he began to cross the street when the red light for pedestrians was showing and a car driver had to swerve to avoid hitting him and crashed into me. I was almost completely crumpled!

Luckily, the driver was unharmed but there was quite a lot of damage done to the car itself. And everybody else around had to quickly get out of the way. It was quite alarming because there were mothers with babies in prams, children holding hands and old people with walking sticks, all waiting to get across the road.

Of course it could have been a lot worse, but let it be a warning to you children, never to cross the road unless the 'little green man' is lit up.

The Pelican Crossing 2

It's the pelican crossing here again! I've been straightened out since the accident and I feel much better again now. I must tell you what I saw today.

It was the end of school. Lots of children leave the school and have to cross the road by me. I know most of the children by name as they often chat to me as they wait for the 'green man' to light up.

Monica often crosses by herself as she walks more slowly than the others. Today, she arrived last as usual and, as she waited for the 'green man', a car drew up and the driver leaned out of his window and said, "Climb in, little girl, I'll take you home."

I held my breath as I waited for her to reply — I could see she was feeling tired and she had a lot of books to carry. It was not her father or anybody she knew and when at last Monica did reply I heaved a great sigh of relief as she said, "No thank you, I prefer to walk, thank you."

The man drove away quickly and I was very proud of Monica. What a sensible girl she is, she understands that you should never accept lifts from strangers, and I hope you do too.

Rosa and the Surveyors

Deep in the forest stood a little house where an old witch lived. She had a friendly, rosy face and was therefore known as Rosa.

The animals of the wood were her friends as she had often helped them in the past. She knew lots of herbal remedies and could therefore make lots of ointments.

One day, when Rosa was collecting herbs at the edge of the wood, she saw several men doing strange things. One of them was peering through a piece of equipment that stood on three legs and was calling out figures as he worked. Another man was writing these figures down, and the third man was measuring. Whatever was going on?

Rosa crept up near to the men in order to listen in on their conversation. Almost at once she realised that they were land surveyors. They were discussing building a road through the wood.

Rosa was furious. A road would mean noise and, furthermore, it would bring danger to her animal friends — she must prevent the road being built at all costs! How fortunate that she was a witch and could therefore cast spells! She muttered, "Frogs legs, change round, change round!" Immediately the numbers on the plan changed round and became muddled. The men, however, did not notice this and packed up all their equipment and went away.

A few days later they returned and began to take measurements again, and again Rosa was on the spot to cast another spell — this time she bewitched the measuring stick. The men shook their heads in disbelief, they measured and measured again but still they could not get them right. In the end they gave up and went away. They came several more times and each time Rosa was there to cast the spells — "This wood is jinxed," the surveyors said to one another in the end, "it's impossible to obtain correct measurements here, let's build the road somewhere else." They drove away, leaving Rosa hiding in the bush, delighted that the wood was to be left in peace.

The Sleepy Meadow

As the sun goes down, the flowers in the meadow close their petals and fall asleep. The ladybirds hide away and the snails go to sleep in their little shells. The birds too, stop chirping and go to bed.

Darkness encroaches very softly. High in the sky, the stars shine and twinkle and sometimes a shooting star falls to the earth and whoever sees it can make a wish.

Fly Catching

Stan sits happily in his arm chair reading his newspaper and drinking a pint of beer. Then suddenly a fly appears to disturb his peace.

The fly buzzes around his head, sits on his nose, flies off and then returns seconds later to sit on his spectacles. Stan then fetches a fly-swatter and chases after the fly.

"Gotcha!" he cries with delight only to find he's smashed his beer glass onto the floor and the beer is spilling all over the carpet. Stan tries to swat the fly again, only this time he hits his newspaper instead. The fly then perches up on the top of the curtain pelmet.

Stan fetches a stool and climbs up to reach the fly. "Smack!" he shouts as he hits the fly, and then Stan loses his balance and falls flat on his face. The fly just flies off and sits on the window sill on a plant pot. Stan lashes out at the fly again "Pow!" and the plant pot smashes to the floor!

"What on earth has been going on in here?" his wife asks on entering the room. "Just look at the state of this room!" "I've been trying to catch a fly," says Stan defensively. "What fly then? I can't see a fly anywhere," says his wife angrily.

In fact, the fly had disappeared through the open door when Stan's wife had come in — what a lot of chaos that fly had caused!

The Little Digger

Every morning when Mr Larkin went to work he had to walk past a building site. There were mounds of earth, lots of machinery and a wooden fence there and so Mr Larkin had to make a detour around the site and this annoyed him so much that he would mutter to himself, "Stupid building site! It's such a nuisance! Makes me go out of my way!"

On the building site there was a little digger, who heard Mr Larkin complaining every day. "Soon there'll be a beautiful new house here, why does he complain so much?" wondered the digger to itself.

So the next time Mr Larkin went past, the little digger decided he would teach him a lesson. The digger lifted Mr Larkin up into the air by his shirt collar. "Let go of me, let go!" screeched Mr Larkin. But the little digger swung him round and round the building site before putting him down on the ground. Once on firm land again, Mr Larkin straightened out his suit, picked up his briefcase and set off for work at once.

From then on he never again complained when he had to make a detour around a building site. He had learnt his lesson well!

Peter in the Rain

It is May. Outside it is pouring with rain. Peter hears his mother talking to the neighbour about the rain. "Oh it's good when it rains in May, for the May rain makes everything grow well!" Peter listened carefully to what his mother said. He would love to grow because his sister was always saying he could not play with her because he was too small, as she was his elder, bossy sister. He sneaked out of the house secretly and went out into the rain.

After a short while, Peter's mother began to wonder where he was. When she looked out of the window she spotted Peter standing in the pouring rain. "Peter!" she cried. "Come in at once. You're absolutely soaked, you'll catch cold standing outside in this weather." Peter shouted back, "I can't come in yet, I need to grow a bit more." Hearing this his mother realized why he was standing outside in the May rain and so she brought him inside.

"The May rain makes all plants, trees, grass and flowers grow well but not children. Children need to eat milk and meat and to get lots of sleep to grow well!" she explained to Peter. Peter was bitterly disappointed, he'd have loved to have grown quickly by standing outside in the May rain! Now he would have to eat less of his favourite food which was chocolate cake, and eat more liver which he hated!

What's Ringing?

When we were young, my sister and I and our two cousins used to spend our holidays at our Grandmother's house. There was a lovely orchard there and we loved to play amongst the trees, making up new games. We especially loved to stay there as we could all sleep together in one huge bedroom. So bedtime at Grandma's was always great fun and we even looked forward to going to bed when we were on holiday!

One day, Connie, the youngest of all, had told Grandma that we had eaten three unripe pears. Grandma was very angry with us for eating the pears without her knowing. So we all decided to get our own back on Connie for telling on us.

That night, we lay in bed and pretended to be asleep. But really we were just waiting until Connie fell asleep. Soon enough she was fast asleep, so we crept up to her and carefully tied a little bell onto her big toe! Connie didn't stir while we did this. We hopped back to bed and laughed to ourselves when she moved and the bell tinkled. At one point she woke up, but then she fell back to sleep, without seeing the bell on the end of her toe. Soon after, we all fell asleep too.

What a row there was in the morning, when Connie woke up to find the bell tied to her big toe! She yelled and screamed at us for playing such a joke on her and then she went off in a sulk for the rest of the day!

Egg-Head

Every Thursday the egg seller would drive down our street in his little car. He would park at the edge of the road and would ring a bell so that all the housewives would come out of their houses to buy fresh eggs.

His car was packed so full with egg boxes that the egg seller only just had enough room to fit into the car. Wherever you looked you could see nothing but eggs, row upon row, pile upon pile of egg boxes! He sold very large eggs at cheap prices.

Once I said to him, "You must be a very careful driver, because if ever you had to put on your brakes suddenly the eggs would break and go all over the place!" He laughed at that and said, "Don't worry, I'll take care, I'm used to driving carefully."

One day, however, he was very unfortunate. He turned down a street, and a car pulled out of a side street without checking first to see if the way was clear. There would have been a might y collision had the egg seller not suddenly braked. He braked hard and scraped a garden fence and then he came to a standstill. The other car was undamaged, but the poor egg seller had egg all over his face, his suit, his shoes, the car seats, and his hair were all streaked with egg! He looked ridiculous and said, "Now, I really have got egg on my face!"

Mike Loses His Mother

Mike goes shopping with his mother to the supermarket. His mother pushes the shopping trolley searching for what she wants to buy. Mike walks by her side and then decides to have a good look round, because there is always something new to see in this huge shop.

Today he discovers a colourful parrot that screeches, "Stand still, and look at this marvellous new window cleaner!" Mike is fascinated because the parrot looks so real. He stops to watch, whilst his mother carries on with her shopping. Mike looks round suddenly — his mother has gone!

Shocked and a little frightened, he walks up and down looking for his mother, and is about to burst into tears when a friendly shop assistant says to him, "Hello, little boy, have you lost your Mummy? Don't cry now, we'll soon find her for you, it happens every day here, it's not so bad as it seems."

Then she takes Mike into a room with a large window down one side so that people can see into the shop. A man was sitting at a desk and the sales assistant says to him, "Call out the little boy's name please, he's lost his mother." So the man speaks through the microphone and says, "Would Mike's mother please come and collect him from the office." The request is heard throughout the shop on the loud speaker system, and Mike's mother is very relieved when she hears it. Straight away she went to the office where Mike is and says, "What a good job I've found you, I've been looking all over for you. Isn't it lucky that these people know about little boys and girls who lose their Mummys!"

At The Doctor's

Claudia put on her father's white shirt, placed a teaspoon behind her ear, put some plasters in her bag and called out, "The consultation hour has begun." Then the patients started to file in one by one, for today Claudia is the Doll's Doctor.

Sabine brought her doll to Claudia, "My doll Susie will not eat, and she's so cold all the time. Please do something for her." Doctor Claudia examined the doll and said, "Your doll has a tummy bug, if she drinks camomile tea for three days she'll soon get better." And Sabine then left, carrying the prescription carefully so as not to ruffle it up.

Then Robert went in with his teddy bear that had a hole in its leg where the filling was spilling out. Claudia gave him a plaster to put over the hole. So Robert went away feeling very relieved that his teddy would soon be better. Next Claudia examined Ursula's black dolly who had a very sore throat, and gave her some lozenges to soothe it. Ursula went away feeling glad that her dolly's throat would soon be better.

The consultation hour with the Doll's Doctor was over and Claudia said, "Same time again tomorrow."

Now she just had time to put her father's shirt back in his wardrobe before he came home from work, and to put the teaspoon back in the cutlery drawer, before her mother noticed that it was not there.

The Butterfly

It was a lovely sunny Summer's day. A beautiful butterfly hopped from flower to flower. A little girl ran up to the butterfly and asked, "I haven't seen you all Winter, did you spend the Winter in the South like the swallows?"

"No," replied the butterfly, "I spent the Winter here in the garden in a cocoon."

"What's a cocoon?" asked the little girl.

"It's a sort of web that I was sleeping in during the Winter until the Spring woke me. Then I came out of the cocoon."

"Who made the cocoon then?" asked the little girl.

"I made it myself when I was still a caterpillar," came the reply.

"You were once a hairy caterpillar then?" asked the little girl in disbelief. "Where did the caterpillar come from?"

"The caterpillar comes from a butterfly egg, and I was a very greedy caterpillar eating all the leaves I could find until I became a chrysalis in the Autumn, or a cocoon as it is also called."

"You've changed a lot in your life," said the little girl, "but I like you best of all as you are now."

"That may well be, but this is my last change as I'm nearly at the end of my life. That's why I must lay lots of eggs so that there'll be lots of butterflies in the future."

Then the butterfly fluttered his wings and flew off leaving the little girl deep in thought. It was a great shame that the butterfly hadn't got long to live when it was such a pretty creature!

Three Little Piglets

Our neighbour has three little piglets. They are still very small and have no mother.

Yesterday evening it was very cold, so they pressed close together and fell asleep. But soon the one that was on the outside woke up feeling cold and swapped places with his brother, so that he was now in the middle and could get warm.

A little later, the other piglet on the outside woke up feeling cold and wanted to be the warm one in the middle. It stood up and pressed itself between the other two so that he could get warm.

But it wasn't long before one of the piglets on the outside became cold and wanted to change places with the piglet in the middle in order to get warm.

This happened again and again throughout the evening, until the farmer's wife came out of the house because she had been watching the piglets changing places. She said to them, "You poor little piglets, you're all freezing, you must be missing your mother."

Then she placed a warm woollen blanket over the three piglets and they soon fell fast asleep. They slept soundly for the rest of the night because now all three of them were warm and snug under the woollen blanket, and not just the piglet in the middle!

Tall Stories

There was once a Princess who really enjoyed making up ridiculous tales and fooling the whole town with them.

One day the King said to her, "My child, it is time that we found you a suitable Prince to marry, for I am growing old and the country needs a new King."

The Princess interrupted at this point and said, "Oh, Daddy all the Princes I know are all really boring! I want a Prince who can tell funny stories and make people laugh better than I can."

The King announced that the Prince who could tell the funniest story would marry the Princess. At once, lots of Princes arrived at the palace and began to tell their stories, but the Princess did not like any of them.

There were three Princes left who wanted to tell their stories, so the Princess said to them, "Which one of you has seen the smallest dwarf in the world?" The first Prince replied, "I know a dwarf that's so small he needs a ladder when he wants to eat soup from a bowl." The second Prince said, "Princess, I know of a dwarf that is so small he can sleep in the shell of a nut." The third Prince said, "Princess, I know of a dwarf that broke his leg when jumping from the carpet to the floor!" The Princess roared with laughter, clapped her hands and shouted, "You shall be my husband and King of this land, because you tell the best funny story!" Soon after, the wedding took place and there was great rejoicing throughout the land.

Kite-Flying

It was a beautiful sunny Autumn day and what's more it was a perfect day for kite-flying. Straight after school, John and Peter took their homemade kite to the meadow behind the school playing-field.

They started flying the kite, holding tight to the string. The wind took the kite high in the sky. "If only I could fly like that," thought John to himself. Then he began to climb up the string until he could get onto the kite. There he sat, on the kite that was only made of thin strips of wood and paper. He could see a long way and he thought how wonderful it was up in the sky, but suddenly the wind dropped and he fell to the ground with a bump.

"I hope that will teach you a lesson in future," said his friend Peter who had been horrified at seeing John climb on to the kite. "You must never try and fly because you are a human being and it's impossible for humans to fly, nor must you try and fly on a kite, they're not strong enough to take your weight. You're very lucky not to have been seriously injured."

Never again did John attempt such a silly stunt.

At the Vet's

In the middle of the wood was a little house, where the vet lived. On this particular day his waiting room was particularly full. The vet called, "Next please," and a deer hobbled into the room. The vet asked, "Why are you limping?" and the deer showed him a piece of glass that was lodged in her left leg. "This happens all the time," said the vet. "People are for ever leaving litter and bottles in the wood after their picnics and then all the animals injure themselves." Then he removed the piece of glass and bandaged her leg.

The next patient was a hare who had terrible stomach ache. He explained that he had tried some of the food that the visitors to the wood had left behind and then he had got stomach pains. So the vet gave him some medicine and told him never to eat unusual food again, since it was not food for hares.

The next patient was a fox who could hardly stand up. The vet was convinced that the fox was drunk — because he'd drunk the contents of a beer bottle that had been left in the wood. "Sleep off your hangover and never drink from unknown bottles again," said the vet to the fox.

Then came a squirrel that had cut its foot on a tin can. The vet treated the squirrel for his wound and warned it never to go near tin cans again, since they had sharp edges which could cut an animal's paws very badly.

The very last patient was a woodpecker that had hurt its beak by tapping too hard on the bark of the tree.

"You're the only animal that hasn't been injured through the carelessness of human beings who can't be bothered to put their rubbish into litter bins when they've been for a day out in the countryside," said the vet sadly.

The Imp

Martin always does his homework as soon as he gets in from school. He shows his mother his work when he's finished and if she is happy with it, then she allows him to play in the garden for a little while longer.

For several days now, his mother has been extremely unhappy with his homework and has found lots of careless errors in his work. "A little imp who makes mistakes is in my school bag," said Martin to his mother. "Oh yes!" said his mother in disbelief and thought nothing more of it. But since Martin still made as many mistakes in his homework a few days later, his mother decided to have a look in his school bag and, there, in the bottom of the bag was a small red imp with a long tail.

"Who are you then?" asked Martin and his mother at the same time. "I'm an imp that makes mistakes," said the imp, "but now that you've discovered me I'm at your service and must rub out all the mistakes in your homework. That is an old imp law. I will serve you only as long as you do not tell anybody else of my existence." Martin thought this was amazing and, from then on, his homework was perfect because the imp would rub out all the mistakes for him.

One day, however, Martin couldn't keep the secret to himself any more and so he told his best friend about the imp. At that exact moment, the imp disappeared, never to be seen again. Since then, Martin has had to check his homework carefully for mistakes, which is altogether much better and more helpful to him and to the teacher.

The Birthday Surprise

Thomas and his father have spent a lot of time whispering to each other recently, as they are planning a birthday surprise for Thomas' mother. The two of them have made a shelf for Thomas' mother that she has been wanting for a long time.

Thomas could hardly wait for it to be his mother's birthday. He kept going up to his mother and asking her, "Mummy, don't you want to know what you're getting for your birthday? Aren't you at all curious to know?" And his mother just laughed and said, "Yes, of course, but I can easily wait until my birthday to find out what my present is."

Unfortunately, Thomas could not wait that long and he gave the secret away one day when he said to his mother, "I'll tell you what you're getting for your birthday — a shelf that Daddy and I have made — but please forget that I told you." Thomas' mother had to laugh at what he had said, but all the same she said, "I can't forget it just like that, you should have kept the secret to yourself, it's not a surprise any more."

Thomas was very disappointed! "Next time, I'll not say a word, I'll keep the secret to myself," thought Thomas.

The Cherry Tree

In Spring, the cherry tree is covered in blossom which has such a lovely scent that it attracts all the bees. They hum and buzz around the tree and take all the pollen away to their hive.

Then all the blossom falls off, and the cherry tree is covered in green leaves. It soon has all the caterpillars around it who love to eat its rich green leaves.

In Summer, the cherry tree is laden with juicy, red cherries. Again, the cherry tree is not alone for long, as the blackbirds love to eat the ripe, red cherries. The children come too and pick the cherries from the tree, and then eat them, but they also hang bunches of them around their ears for fun.

When Autumn comes the wind blows the leaves off the cherry tree, and the swallows gather on its bare branches before they make their long journey south.

Then it's Winter, and it begins to snow and thousands of snowflakes land on the bare branches of the tree. The cherry tree is very happy that it has so many visitors because then it is never bored or lonely any time of the year.

The Big Turnip

There was once a farmer who had a turnip field. One turnip, however, was much larger than the others — it grew and grew and just kept on growing. In the end it filled a huge cart which two oxen could just about manage to pull.

The farmer presented the turnip to the King as a gift. The King was astonished at the size of the turnip as he'd never seen such a huge turnip before. When the King heard that the farmer was poor, he gave him some land, meadows and cattle in return for the turnip.

Now it so happened that the farmer had a brother who was very rich. When he heard of his brother's good fortune, he was very envious and so he decided that he, too, would present the King with a gift.

He chose his finest horse and took it to the palace. The King accepted the horse as a gift and because he knew the farmer was rich he said to him, "I have something extra special for you in return. I present you with the huge turnip." So the rich farmer had to take the turnip which had brought his brother such good fortune, back home with him. Next time, perhaps, he would not be so greedy.

The Ghost Story

Sebastian is a real book worm. He loves reading more than anything else in the world. He reads for hours on end, and forgets all about everything else. He reads in the bath, in bed, and even secretly at school behind the desk when the teacher is not looking.

His favourite stories are ghost stories. One night, before falling asleep he had read a scary tale of a ghost that could not rest and so it wandered around haunting people.

In the middle of the night Sebastian was woken up by a strange sound. He could hear someone scratching at the window. He went to wake his mother, "Mummy, there's a g-g-g-ghost at my window!" When Sebastian's mother looked out of the window she said, "Oh, Sebastian, it's only a branch of the maple tree knocking against the window."

Sebastian was very relieved to hear this and went back to bed contented with this explanation. His mother turned out the light and said, "That will teach you to read such scary ghost stories just before you go to sleep, Sebastian."

The Milk Churn

Every year young David would spend several weeks of the Summer holidays at his grandparents' home up in the mountains. He loved the fresh mountain air and spent most of his time outside with the animals.

His grandparents weren't farmers but their next door neighbour, John, was a farmer, and David had grown very fond of all the farm animals over the years. But he loved the cows best of all.

One day his grandfather gave him a picture of a farm and its animals. All David had to do was to cut out all the pictures and then he could make his very own farm. David set to work at once, cutting out the pictures and sticking them onto the card. Then he came to his favourite animal — the cow. He began to cut out the black and white cow very carefully, but he had an accident just as he'd nearly finished cutting it out. He had

accidentally cut off the cow's tail. David burst into tears and went running to his grandmother. "Grandma, I've cut off the tail! What shall I do now?" he wailed. But try as she did, she could not console young David. He was so distressed that his temperature soared and he had to go to bed, but he slept badly that night.

When he awoke the next morning he felt as though it had all been a bad dream. But there at his bedside stood the next door neighbour, John, holding a calf in his hands. "Look, I've brought you this calf. It's yours. She's called Elsa and when she's fully grown she'll produce milk and this is your very own milk churn."

David jumped out of bed at once and was thrilled with his presents. It wasn't long before he'd completely forgotten his upset of the day before!

The Sad Fairy

A little fairy lived among the water lilies in the lake in the middle of the forest. She lived on her own and was very lonely. Often she would be found crying though no-one knew why. She was never happy. The flowers could not make her happy nor could the birds' singing. The deer who went to drink at the edge of the lake looked at the fairy's sad eyes but he couldn't make her smile either. Every day a pair of birds would visit the lake regularly. The fairy would watch them play together. They were such tiny birds, much smaller than the other birds in the forest. One day the fairy went up and spoke to the two birds and discovered that they lived in a distant pine forest. The birds came to the lake each day because they wanted to see the fairy smile. The little fairy listened and watched the two birds but still she did not smile.

One day, the birds brought the fairy a present, a grain of millet that shone like gold in the Summer sun. The fairy was delighted to accept the present and for the first time ever, she smiled. To thank the birds she touched the heads of the two birds and, at that moment, the top of their heads turned a golden colour. From that day on, the birds have been known as 'Goldcrests'. We do not see these tiny birds very often because they spend most of their time with the little fairy at the edge of the lake.

The Moonflower

The bluebell, Bonnie, dreamt of going to the moon. Whenever there was a full moon in the middle of Summer she longed to be on the moon, to know what it was really like up there, high in the sky. She'd like to go there, just once in her life.

The moon heard her plea and so one evening, when Bonnie was fast asleep, he pulled her up to him. When she woke up the next morning she had no idea where she was for a moment and then suddenly she realised that she was sitting on the moon! Her wish had come true!

The moon smiled at her, "Now, little bluebell, you can see for yourself what it's like being on the moon!" Bonnie looked around and saw a few clouds and several stars, but nothing else. There were no flowers, no trees, no bees and no noise.

Bonnie was the only living creature on the moon. She began to shiver with cold, for there were no warm rays of sunshine here. The moon realised that the bluebell could not stay with him in the moon because she needed the sun to live. So the moon said to the bluebell, "I think it would be best if I sent you back to earth, to your own garden, because you cannot survive here without the sun."

No sooner said than done. A little cloud took Bonnie gently back to earth. The other flowers were overjoyed to have her back with them. She, too, was very happy to be back among her friends, the beetles and snails, the grasshoppers and the bees. And she told them all what it had been like when she was a Moonflower.

Dancing in the Kitchen

At midnight the cutlery drawer sprang to life. "We've been so bored lately, let's dance!" said the forks. "Yes, let's!" replied the knives and spoons. So they all leapt up onto the kitchen table and began to dance. "We'll make the music," said the wooden spoon, drumming on the large saucepan. The whisk spun round and round thoroughly enjoying itself.

One spoon danced with the sieve, the weighing scales danced with the corkscrew and the tin-can danced alone. The large frying pan was too clumsy to dance and so he stood at the edge of the table and tapped in time to the music.

Suddenly, there was an almighty crash as a plate that had been spinning too quickly fell to the floor. The dance was over and all the kitchen equipment made their way back to the shelves and into the drawers. Before long, the kitchen was quiet once again.

The next morning, the housewife entered the kitchen and was puzzled by the pieces of broken crockery lying all over the floor. "I wonder who's broken that plate?" she thought to herself. Of course, she'd never guess in a million years that a dance had taken place in her kitchen the night before.

The Snail's Home

One day, the snail was crawling through the meadow, when a little mouse stopped and asked him, "Are you going on a journey because you're carrying such a big suitcase on your back?" The snail was very offended and retorted, "That's no suitcase, it's my home!"

"Is that a house then? But where are the windows?" demanded the little mouse.

"I don't have, or need windows," replied the snail and continued on its way.

Then an ant stopped, and said to the snail, "I see you're off on holiday, seeing as you're carrying such a huge case on your back." "That's not a case, that's my house!" said the snail angrily. "Where's the chimney then?" asked the ant. "I don't need a chimney," replied the snail and went on his way.

Then the snail met a worm who asked, "Are you the postman, as you're carrying such a huge sack?" "No I'm not the postman and that's no sack, but my house." "Is there any furniture in it then?" asked the curious worm. "No there isn't, and I don't need furniture," retorted the snail.

It wasn't long before it started to rain. All the other animals ran for shelter but the snail just curled up inside his shell.

His shell makes a very comfortable home even though it has no windows or furniture. It keeps him dry and safe from the rain.

Henry Creates a Stir

and white striped trousers. Even the conductor was speechless and dropped his baton in shock when he saw Henry. Henry's appearance ended all the serious singing on that particular evening.

Afterwards all the other frogs decided that they would have trousers like Henry's and ordered them at once from the pixie.

From then on, at least one frog would be late for the singing rehearsal each evening because he would stop and look at his reflections in the lake.

This annoyed the choir leader so much, that he warned the frogs that they would lose their place in the choir if they were ever late again, and furthermore, everyone was to wear green, and so that meant an end to the red and white striped trousers!

The frogs did not want to lose their place in the choir and so they all gave up their lovely stripy trousers and concentrated on their singing once again. From then on, all the frogs sang happily together and never again wore striped trousers!

Henry was a young frog who was not only very proud of his good looks but of his wonderful voice as well. He even sang in the frog choir!

One day, he went along to the tailor's and ordered the tailor (who was a pixie) to make him a pair of trousers in a red and white striped material. Before long the trousers were ready and Henry put them on and walked proudly home in them.

Henry thought of the frog concert that was to take place that evening and how astonished and envious all the other frogs would be. Henry stopped to look at his reflection in the lake, and as he admired how smart he looked he completely forgot the time.

Only when it began to get dark did he suddenly realise that he might not make it to the concert in time. He hurried to the pond where the concert was to take place, then, he heard in the distance the choir singing, without him! He raced to where the choir was and as he appeared, the choir stopped singing and gazed in amazement at Henry in his new red

Why Me?

There was once a little girl who would answer, "Why does it always have to be me?" whenever she was asked to do something.

Her mother was very annoyed with her daughter's attitude and one day she thought of a way to stop her daughter moaning whenever she was asked to do something.

When the little girl came home from school, very hungry one afternoon, she sat down at the kitchen table as usual and noticed that it hadn't been set for tea. She hurried up to the cooker and noticed that no meal had been cooked! Her mother was sitting in the lounge reading the newspaper.

"Mummy, why is there nothing for tea?" asked the little girl. "Why haven't you cooked anything?" "Why does it always have to be me?" replied the mother. The little girl was completely taken aback, as her mother had used her very own words. From then on the little girl very rarely said, "Why does it always have to be me?" and she helped her mother much more in the house.

April Fool!

Have you ever played an April fool joke on anyone? Well, I must tell you of what we did last April 1st. We, being me and my brothers and sisters. It went like this:—

We put a purse on the pavement and tied a piece of string around it. The end of the string was tied to the bedroom window and we leaned out of the window and pulled the string attached to the purse up towards us whenever a passer-by tried to pick up the purse, so that the purse dangled on the end of the string.

Then the passer-by would look up at us and we'd shout "April Fool!" Some of the people were furious at this and shouted back, "You young rascals," but the majority of them would just laugh and then continue on their way. Probably they remembered what they had been like when they were children.

The Way to the Meadow

In the beautiful Austrian mountains, not far from Kufstein there is a beautiful meadow that is called 'Walleralm' by the hill walkers who like to wander along the Alpine paths.

At the beginning of the path to Walleralm there is a fork in the path so the walkers don't know which path to take. The walkers then stop and ask the farmer, the farmer's wife or his children in the near-by farm the way to Walleralm. "It's that way to Walleralm," comes the reply, pointing to the right path.

Because there are so many walkers, especially during the Summer, who do not know which path to take to Walleralm, the family found it hard to get on with their work as they were interrupted every five minutes.

So one day one of the children sat down and began to draw a dwarf with a beard pointing his arm towards Walleralm. Underneath the picture the child wrote, "This way to Walleralm!" and he placed the picture at the fork in the path so that all the walkers would know the way to Walleralm without having to stop and ask the farmer and his children for directions.

Night Workers

It is bed time. Daddy sits at the edge of Ben's bed and says, "Sleep tight my son. The flowers, the trees and the houses and cars are already asleep."

"Does everything and everyone sleep at night, Daddy?" asked Ben sleepily.

"No, not everyone sleeps at night, some people have to work during the night. They work so that we can sleep in peace." "Do they watch over us then?" asked Ben. "Sort of," answered Ben's Daddy. "Just think for a moment of the firemen and policemen who work during the night and who are always alert and ready to help those in need to put out fires and to arrest thieves when we are sleeping. Then there are doctors and nurses who work during the night to care for the sick and seriously injured. They are always ready to cope with accidents and emergencies."

"Trains run through the night, don't they Daddy? so that must mean that some train drivers have to work nights," said Ben. "Yes that's right. There are lots of people who work nights besides those I've already mentioned. For instance, pilots of big aircraft and newspaper people work nights." He then looked down at his son, but he had fallen asleep.

Trick Questions

"There are seven birds sitting on the telephone wire. A man shoots two of them. How many are left?" asked the teacher. Mark thought and thought and then he answered, "There are five left." "Wrong," said the teacher. "There are none left, they all flew away when they heard the gun shots because it frightened the birds." Mark was annoyed, because he'd been caught out by the trick question.

It so happened that in the next mathematics lesson, the teacher said, "There are twenty eggs in a basket. If I lay another two on top, how many eggs are there in the basket?" "Twenty-two," called out one little boy. "No," said Mark, "there are still only twenty in the basket because teachers can't lay eggs!" Mark grinned to himself and thought, "I didn't get caught out that time!"

New Year's Eve

It was New Year's Eve, the last day of the year. Two girls were talking about the days of the year whilst looking at the calendar which only had one leaf left to tear off.

Then their little brother came up to them, and they said to him, "Oh dear, poor little Johnny, you've as many noses on your face as there are days in the year!" Johnny was very worried when they said this and so he peered at his reflection in the mirror but couldn't see any more noses than one.

His big sisters burst out laughing at this point and said, "There's only one day left of the year, and that's how many noses you have just the one!"

Johnny was very relieved to hear this and he went off to quickly try out this new joke on his Mother seeing as it would only work on that one day of the year New Year's Eve.

The Swallow

One Autumn day, the baby swallow saw the squirrel collecting nuts and acorns to hide away in his home and in various places in the wood. "Why are you doing that?" asked the swallow. "I'm seeing that I have enough food to last me through the cold Winter because when the ground is frozen I can't find any food," replied the squirrel. "So if I hide stores of food in lots of places, then I will have enough food to last the whole of the Winter."

Hearing this, the young swallow returned to the nest, taking some flies that he caught on the way home with him. He gave them all to his mother and said, "I've been collecting lots of food so that we won't go hungry in the cold Winter months."

"Oh you silly thing!" replied the swallow's mother, "we don't need to store food for the Winter because we fly to the south where it is warm. There's plenty of food there, that's one of the reasons why we go there — for food and warmth." "Then why doesn't the squirrel come with us then?" asked the silly young swallow. At this, his mother roared with laughter. Do you know why?

Visit to the Zoo

For a birthday treat Peter's parents took him to the zoo. It was Peter's very first visit to the zoo and he was very excited about seeing all the animals. Peter ran from one cage to another to see all the different animals. There were lions lazing in the sun, playful chimpanzees, penguins looking like men in evening suits, camels, tigers and many more besides. It was great fun at the zoo!

When he became worn out from running around so much, Peter went and rested on the terrace of the cafe. It was a boiling hot day and the flies were attracted to the terrace by the scent of lemonade. A fat man sat at one of the tables and tried to swat the flies that were annoying him using his beer mat as a fly swatter. He waved the mat at the flies, but one time he leaned too far backwards and fell off his chair. It was such a funny sight that everyone roared with laughter and in the end even the man had to laugh at himself.

After this rest, Peter continued to look around the zoo with his parents. They saw elephants, giraffes and zebras and many more animals besides before they went home.

That night when Peter was in bed, his mother asked him what he'd enjoyed seeing the most. Peter answered that he had loved the animals, but most of all he'd enjoyed seeing the fat man fall off his chair. Then he closed his eyes and smiled as he thought about the fat man falling off the chair as he tried to swat a fly.

The New Doll

It was Jane's sixth birthday and she received lots of lovely presents from her parents and sister. A jigsaw, a painting book and a brightly coloured ball were just three of the presents she was lucky enough to receive on her birthday.

Auntie Ann came to the house in the afternoon to give Jane her birthday present. As soon as Jane was given the present she tore off the wrapping paper to reveal a lovely doll with eyes that looked almost real, dressed in a gown of the finest silk.

"Thank you very much, Auntie Ann," said Jane and she held the doll very carefully because she was afraid it might break if she dropped it. Then she put the doll on a chair and that is where it stayed for the rest of the day.

In the evening, Jane was worn out from the excitement of the day and during tea she began to look very sleepy, so her mother put her to bed and asked, "Do you want to take your new dolly to bed with you?" Jane replied, "No thanks," and then, she pulled out her old shabby rag doll from beneath the pillow and held her tightly in her arms. "I see you really care for the old rag doll that you've had since you were a baby. What a good job that Auntie Ann can't see you now!" It just goes to show that the old familiar toys are best.

Land of the Silly

The King of the Land of the Silly was old and tired of being King. So, as he had no son to inherit his title and kingdom, he decided it was time to elect a new King. He realized that he must elect the silliest of his subjects to be the new King.

Lots of people presented themselves at the palace and each one had to answer a question that the King put to them. In the King's opinion they were all too clever to be King, and were not silly enough to inherit his title.

Then one day, three tradesmen came to the palace and they all looked so silly that the King was very hopeful that one of them might just be silly enough to be the new King.

"The question is this, if the palace were on fire, what would you do?" asked the King.

The first fellow answered, "Your Majesty, it's quite simple. I'd ask all the women in the kingdom to come and sew a gigantic blanket that could be thrown over the fire to put it out." The King was indeed pleased with such a silly suggestion.

He then turned to the second fellow, who answered, "Your Majesty, I would blow on the fire until it went out!" The King was delighted at such a silly idea and he turned to the third fellow who replied, "Your Majesty, I would take a sieve to the well, fill it with water and then I'd pour the water over the fire to put it out." The King cried, "You're the silliest person in the land! You will be the new King!" And the whole land celebrated and rejoiced for three days at the choice of the new silly King.

The Wild Rose

A long time ago, Mary, Joseph and baby Jesus were fleeing from Bethlehem to Egypt to escape the wicked King Herod who wanted to kill all the baby boys in the land. They journeyed by night and hid during the day, because King Herod wanted to kill baby Jesus.

One morning Mother Mary washed Jesus' shirt and lay it out over a thorn bush to dry. Later on, when she went to see whether it was dry, she was amazed to see lots of green leaves and pink and white coloured roses on the thorn bush. A perfumed scent filled the air.

"Jesus has made this happen," said Mary to the bush. "It is his way of thanking you for your help." Since then, roses have bloomed every year on the thorn bush and they are known as wild roses.

In the Evening

In the evening the sun said, "I'm tired, it's been such a long day, I'm going to sleep now." And then she sank behind the mountains.

The flowers then nodded their heads and said, "If the sun isn't going to shine anymore, then we might as well go to sleep too," and so they closed up their petals and slept.

Then the bees said, "If the flowers have closed up their petals and gone to bed, then it's time for us to sleep too." In the meadow, the hares scratched their long ears and hopped back to their burrows to go to sleep.

Soon everyone was fast asleep and when the moon shone that night, it was contented that everyone was sleeping peacefully. Only the hedgehog could be heard from time to time rustling in the undergrowth.

Swinging

Emma's father attached a swing to the branch of the pear-tree for Emma's seventh birthday. She was delighted with her present and loved to sit and swing all day long. She swings back and forth until the wind whistles past her ears and she almost reaches the top branches of the tree.

Today, Emma has swung so much and so high, that she even reached the clouds! She whizzed past the mountains, over dark forests and over calm seas, further and further she swung — and then she heard her friend's voice calling, "Emma it's me, can you hear me?"

Hearing her friend's voice so loud and clear, Emma awoke from her daydream and thought to herself, "What a pity I've been woken from my daydream, I was enjoying swinging so high and far away. I'd have liked to have swung even further and to have talked to the wind!"

The Forgetful Squirrel

There was once a young squirrel that was so forgetful that his parents were very worried about his future. No sooner had they taught him how to use his bushy tail to balance when jumping than he would forget it as soon as they had finished explaining it to him. So, then they would have to teach him all over again. He would even forget how to carry nuts between his paws.

"How ever will you cope on your own?" they would ask him every day. The little squirrel was making his parents go grey with worry.

When the young squirrel was fully grown, he had to fend for himself. In the Autumn he managed to collect lots of nuts and acorns and he stored them in a safe place so he would have enough to eat during the cold Winter months. Then he went to sleep for the Winter.

He woke up a few months later, feeling very hungry and went off into the wood in search of his stores of food. He searched and searched but could not find his food stores anywhere in the wood. The food was not to be found behind the bush, nor was it behind the hedge.

In desperation, he asked some of the other animals that lived in the wood where he had stored his food for the Winter. None of them could remember where the young squirrel had stored his food. In the end the squirrel decided to ask the wise old owl if he knew where he had hidden his store of food. The wise owl replied, "Yes, young squirrel, I know where your store of food is, I watched you hide it in the roots of the old oak tree, on the other side of the wood." The squirrel was overjoyed to hear this and thanked the wise owl for his help. He then scuttled off to the old oak tree and found his store of food.

The Toad

Roger is a young rascal. He's always playing jokes on people, and what's more he very rarely gets found out!

One day he placed a very special present on his little sister's desk. It was a little box and because his sister, Maria, is very nosy she opened the box to see what was inside. "Oh! help, it's a frog!" cried Maria so loudly that her mother came running into the room. Roger also rushed into the room and pretended to be very surprised at seeing a frog!

"That's not a frog, it's a toad," said Maria's mother. "Ugh, it's horrible whatever it is," replied Maria. "I agree it's not a pretty animal but just look at its big gentle eyes! Besides, toads eat snails and insects and other creepy crawlies, which gardeners are very thankful for," Maria's mother remarked.

"But tell me, how did the toad get here?" asked Maria's mother. She glared at Roger, but he just shrugged his shoulders and looked innocent. Then he looked sheepishly at the ground and could not bear to look his mother in the eye anymore. "I know you are responsible for this, Roger, so you can just go and put it back in the garden where it belongs!" said his mother, who could always tell when her son was guilty.

Hearing Things

Mr Johnson is a placid, hardworking man and has led a very quiet life.

It so happened that one evening, Mr Johnson turned on his television set as usual, only to hear the newsreader say, "Good evening, Mr Johnson. Here are tonight's headlines." "Well, well, whatever next!" thought Mr Johnson to himself. "Did he really say my name then? Perhaps he knows me?"

Then he poured out a glass of beer and settled down to watch the television. It was not long before the newsreader called out from the television, "Cheers, Mr Johnson!" just as he took a sip of beer. "I must be dreaming," thought Mr Johnson to himself. "I'd better go to the doctor's, I must have been over-working again."

A little later on, Mr Johnson was watching a pop programme. Just as a singer was in the middle of a very dramatic song, the telephone started to ring. The pop star stopped singing at once and said to Mr Johnson, "Go and answer the telephone, Mr Johnson, the ringing is putting me off my singing." Mr Johnson thought he must be going completely mad when he heard this. So he answered the telephone, but it was a wrong number. Then, he returned to his armchair to watch the television again.

The pop programme was followed by an exciting film, to end the evening's viewing. As Mr Johnson settled down to watch it, he forgot the events of earlier that evening. At the end of the film he heard a friendly voice say, "That's all for this evening of the 1st April, we wish you all a Good Night, especially Mr Johnson — April Fool!"

The Pelican Crossing 3

Do you remember me? I'm the pelican crossing and I've already told you two stories. Well, here's another one.

This story happened last night. Suddenly I saw a little child approaching in his night gown. He looked about three years old and he had bare feet. I thought it very odd indeed.

Then I saw Mrs Miller coming round the corner to the crossing. (She works as a waitress in a restaurant and always finishes very late at night.) When she saw the little boy she looked astonished and asked, "Simon whatever are you doing here?" and she led him away by the hand.

I'd never have found out the rest of the story if I hadn't overheard two ladies discussing it the next day. "You'll never guess what, but Mrs Miller's little boy crept out secretly last night to meet her from work, wearing only his night gown!

He had woken up and wondered where his mummy was. He went downstairs to ask his daddy and instead of going back up to bed, he decided he'd go to meet her from work. He started to get very frightened out in the night all by himself, but luckily his mother found him before he wandered too far.

What a good job she found him, otherwise she'd have had a terrible shock when she got home and discovered his bed empty!" said one woman to the other.

The Pipe

Achmed was the son of a wealthy Arab trader. For the first time ever, Achmed was allowed to accompany his father with the camel caravan this year. Once a year, his father would go on the long journey to a distant port to sell silk and muslin.

Each evening when the travellers reached an oasis surrounded by palm trees they would put up their tents and camp the night there. And when the sun went down the Muslims would get out their prayer mats, bow to Mecca three times, and thank Allah for a good day. Then the men would sit outside the tents and smoke their pipes before going to bed.

It seemed to young Achmed that smoking the pipe gave the men great pleasure. They all appeared to enjoy smoking their pipes very much. Achmed wanted to try it too, but was not allowed because he was too young.

One evening, however, the men had to go down to the watering hole to check that the camels were well settled for the night. Achmed seized his chance and went into the tent to smoke the pipe. "Ugh," he said as he tried to smoke the pipe, "it tastes horrible." Achmed turned green and felt sick when he tasted the pipe, and then he saw his father standing at the entrance to the tent. "Well, well my son, you only learn from experience and trying things out for yourself!" said Achmed's father as he looked down at his young son.

The young boy decided that he would wait until he was a little older before he joined the men in their pipe smoking!

The Real Princess

There was once a Prince who wanted to marry a genuine Princess. He journeyed throughout the land and met many Princesses, but he found fault with them all. So, not finding a Princess that he wanted to marry, he returned home, very disappointed.

One evening there was a terrible storm. There was thunder and lightning and it poured with rain. Someone knocked at the door of the palace and there on the doorstep stood a Princess, but she looked more like a drowned rat than a Princess!

She said she was a real Princess, so the Prince decided to find out if she was telling the truth. He placed a pea under the mattress of the bed in which she was to sleep, then he lay twenty mattresses on top of it, and then twenty feather pillows on top of the mattresses.

The next morning, the Prince asked the Princess how she had slept. "Oh I slept really badly," she moaned. "I slept on something really hard which gave me a terrible pain!" This answer showed that she was indeed a real, true Princess. Only a true Princess could be so sensitive that she could feel a pea through twenty mattresses and twenty feather pillows.

The Prince asked the Princess to marry him, and she accepted.

The whole kingdom rejoiced at the marriage of the Prince and Princess and they lived happily ever after.

The Prescription

A long time ago, a farmer went to the chemist shop carrying a wooden door with him. The chemist looked at the man in amazement as he heaved the door into his shop. "You've come to the wrong place, the joiner is three doors down the road!" said the chemist to the farmer.

The farmer replied, "No I've come to the right place," and he explained that his wife was ill and that the doctor had given her a prescription.

Since there was no paper, pen or ink at home, only a piece of chalk, the doctor had written the prescription on the door with a piece of chalk. "So this is the prescription, please make it up for me now, Mr Chemist," said the farmer, handing over the prescription.

The chemist quickly made up the medicine for the farmer's wife and the farmer went happily home.

The Tale of the Robber

A little boy told me this story and asked me to write it down for other children to read.

"There was once a wicked robber who stole diamonds, money and gold; in fact, anything he thought was valuable.

One day he was stealing a coffee grinder, the police caught him in the act and put him in prison. Then a fairy came along and cast a spell on the robber so that he was freed. From then on he was a good man and never stole again."

What do you think of the story? Wouldn't it be wonderful if all wicked people could be made good so easily?

The Crock of Tears

There was once a lady whose only child died. She wept bitterly every night at his grave, and no one could console her.

Then one night she saw a procession of children pass by in the sky and she noticed one of them wore a night gown that was wet through and he was carrying a crock filled with water. The crock must have been very heavy because the child was trailing behind the others. When they reached a fence, the other children hopped over it easily, while he stood still and just looked at it.

The mother recognised this child as her own son and went to help him over the fence. The boy said, "I have to carry this heavy crock, which is filled with your tears. Look how wet my shirt is? Please don't cry anymore, then I can join in with the other children." From then on, the child's mother shed no more tears.

The Hippopotamus

There was once a hippopotamus called Harry who nibbled all day long. He spent all his pocket money on sweets and toffees. Of course he began to put on weight, but what was worse, he suffered from very bad toothache. The pain became so severe that he went off sweets and decided he really ought to go to the dentist.

The dentist knew at once that Harry's teeth had not been properly looked after. He had to stand on a stool to examine Harry's large mouth and he soon found the cause of the pain; a back tooth with an enormous hole in it. That would have to be filled! He gave Harry an injection so that he would not feel the pain and then he began to drill.

Harry struggled and complained bitterly, but the dentist was not put off by his moaning. The dentist needed a lot of cement to fill the hole.

When the dentist had finished filling Harry's tooth, he said, "You must not eat anything for three days, as it will take that long for the cement to set properly.

I think you should give up eating sweets for good and take care of your teeth properly in future. You must brush your teeth regularly every night and every morning and after meals. If you do that then you will have healthy teeth and won't need to come and see me quite so often.

If you don't do as I suggest then I'll have to take that tooth out next time." The thought of losing a tooth petrified poor Harry hippopotamus and he resolved never to eat sweets again. In fact since then he has been eating lots of vegetables!

The Dustbin Men

Jimmy has just had his third birthday. Every Friday morning, he waits at the garden gate for the dustbin men. They come every Friday in a bright green lorry to empty the bins.

Jimmy is amazed by the way the men stand at the back of the wagon and jump off when the lorry stops. They carry the dustbins full of rubbish on their shoulders and then tip it into the lorry.

Today, Jimmy says to his Mother, "Mummy, I want to be a dustbin man when I grow up."

His sister wrinkles up her nose in disgust and says, "Ooh, but rubbish smells so awful!" Their mother replies, "We should be very grateful that there are dustbin men, just imagine the amount of waste and smell there'd be without them! Of course, Jimmy can be a dustbin man if he wants."

Then she smiled to herself and thought, "He'll want to be lots of things before he finally makes his mind up."

Cure for Fear

Freddie was a happy little fellow except when he became afraid. He was afraid of storms, afraid of going into the dark cellar alone and even afraid of bursting a balloon! One time, he even ran away from the school's shooting festival because the sound of the guns scared him.

His mother was beginning to despair. So one day she went to the chemist and asked for some tablets that would cure fear. The chemist explained that he could easily cure upset stomachs and headaches with tablets, but he had no tablets to cure fear.

So the mother approached a very clever man who'd read hundreds of books. She asked him if he knew how to cure fear, but he had no helpful suggestion to offer.

As there was nothing more Freddie's mother could do she set off home. On the way she saw a busker at the side of the road playing a mouth organ. He stopped Freddie's mother and asked her why she looked so sad. She told him all about Freddie's problem and the musician declared joyfully that the best cure for fear was music. "Tell your son to sing or whistle the next time he's afraid," he said. She thanked him for this sound advice and hurried home to tell her son the news.

Freddie took the musician's advice and whenever there was thunder and lightning he'd sit and play his recorder, and forget his fear. He whistled when he had to go down the cellar and his fear went away. From then on he was a happy little fellow all the time!

The Great Titmouse

A small bird hops around the garden. It has a black head, a green and white flecked neck and a golden yellow and black striped chest. It is a Great Titmouse. He manages to find enough food to eat all year round, even in Winter, by using his sharply pointed beak to peck into the ground to search for different kinds of food.

Today he flies onto a pear tree and discovers a bird's nest that has been abandoned a long time ago. Deep down inside the nest, the Titmouse spots a batch of butterfly eggs and so he sets to work to reach the eggs.

When he has eaten them he sits back, very content with his morning's work.

The Titmouse loves to have a nice long rest when it has eaten a meal. Then he will go off again in search of some more food. He has a busy afternoon ahead of him.

The Cat's Mail

There was once an old man who lived all alone with his pet cat. One day he was called away urgently and forgot to leave the cat any food as he hurried away.

Suddenly, in the middle of his journey, he remembered his cat. He then thought of a way to send some food to his pet cat. Firstly, he went and bought a piece of fresh fish. He put the fish into an envelope, sealed it, wrote his home address on the envelope and posted it.

The postman posted the package through the letter box, the cat soon smelt the fish and ripped open the envelope using her sharp claws. The cat then ate the fish very greedily since she'd had nothing to eat for two whole days!

At Our Place

A farmer's boy once visited his uncle's farm. As the uncle showed his nephew around the boy was forever finding fault.

He would say, "At our farm the cows produce more milk."

"At our farm the hens lay bigger eggs than yours."

"At our farm the air is much fresher."

After a while the uncle became very irritated by his nephew always saying how much better things were on his farm. So he decided to teach the boy a lesson. He gave his nephew a good slap across the face the next time he began to say "At our farm . . ."

At this the nephew calmly stated, "At our farm you get slapped across the face much harder!" This made the uncle burst out laughing.

The Oven Imp

As the grandmother sat knitting by the window one Spring day, she suddenly heard a noise coming from the oven. She opened the oven door to find a tiny imp with a bright red face looking very angry indeed.

"Why has no one been stoking up the fire?" he asked crossly. "Because of the warm weather I expect," replied the grandmother laughing.

When the oven imp peeped out and saw the sun shining brightly he disappeared as fast as lightning back into the oven. Inside, there was a real racket going on. It wouldn't be cold again for at least five months. Then the fire would be stoked up in the Winter months, which would please the oven imp enormously. He couldn't wait for Winter to arrive.

Who Rides the Donkey?

One day a miller and his son took their donkey to market because they had to sell it in order to buy food for themselves, as they were very poor.

On the way there, they met a group of girls who called out to them, "What a daft lot you are! You're both walking when one of you could be riding on the donkey!" The miller and his son thought this was an excellent idea, so the miller sat his son on the donkey, whilst he walked alongside.

They hadn't gone much further when an old man shouted out, "You should be ashamed of yourself, young man, riding on the donkey whilst your father walks!" The son went bright red when he heard this, and climbed down from the donkey to let his father ride instead.

They hadn't made much progress when a couple called out to them, "What a selfish man you are, riding whilst your son trails behind!" The miller said to his son, "Jump up here son, let's both ride on the donkey."

So the donkey carried them both to the market place. As they approached the market, a passer-by called out, "How can you be so cruel? Don't you realise that you're mistreating your donkey by both riding on his back. Your weight is far too much for your donkey to carry!"

When they heard this they both jumped off the donkey at once. The miller said to his son, "Well son, it's back to square one, back to where we started, with the two of us walking at the side of the donkey!"

The Old Wizard

There was once a wizard who used to like to walk through the streets wearing a brightly coloured cloak and a long pointed hat. He would carry a magic wand in his right hand. Lots of children would run behind him because they thought he looked very funny in his cloak and hat. They would make fun of him.

After a while the wizard could not stand the children jeering at him any more. With a wave of his magic wand he cast a magic spell on the children.

At once, the children were transformed into black and white birds — into swallows. This soon stopped the children from following the wizard and laughing at him!

The Skunk's Story

When God had created all the animals in the world, he called them all around him so that he could bestow a special gift on each one of them.

To the first animal, he said, "You're a lion and I am going to give you strength, sharp teeth and claws." To the second animal, he said, "You're to be known as the elephant and your thick skin and huge size will protect you from danger."

To the third animal, he said, "You're a snake and I'm giving you a poisonous tongue for use in emergencies."

God continued in this way giving out special gifts to the animals. The deer received sharp antlers, the cat good eyes, the dog a keen nose and the hedgehog prickles to protect it from its enemies.

When God had finished giving out the special gifts, an animal that looked a little bit like a big squirrel came rushing up to him at the last minute. "Why are you so late?" asked God. "I've given out all the gifts. But wait, I've got just one left — a terrible stink — which will scare off all your enemies." God presented the skunk with this gift which it was very disappointed with at first, but later he came to value his special gift because it certainly kept his enemies well away, and made him safe.

So now you know why a skunk is usually by itself! No one enjoys being too close to it!

Thanksgiving

It is Autumn. The teacher is telling his pupils about harvesting. The children join in the discussion and tell the teacher all they know of maize, potatoes and fruit. There are a couple of farmers' children in the class and they have plenty to say on this subject.

Finally, the teacher tells of harvest time or thanksgiving, as it is sometimes called, which is always celebrated in the Autumn. It is the occasion when everyone thanks God for bringing in the harvest safely. People take gifts of vegetables and fruit to church.

At that point, a boy put up his hand and asked, "What can I thank God for when I don't do any harvesting? My father isn't a farmer and we don't have a garden." "You can thank God for helping all the farmers to bring in the harvest safely. After all, there is always something you can thank God for," replied the teacher. Now all the class realized they would be able to thank God for the harvest, even though they had not actually harvested anything themselves.

The Talking Mountain

One day a husband and wife received an invitation to a wedding. But because they kept a cow that needed constant looking after, only one of them would be able to go to the wedding. The difficulty was deciding who should go and who should stay.

"You should stay at home," said the wife to her husband. "You often go to town and I have to stay here on my own a lot of the time. I could do with a change and I haven't been to a wedding for simply ages."

"But I think I should go," protested the husband to his wife. "I can't milk the cow very well and besides, I want to see my cousins. I think I should go." They carried on the argument for some time, but couldn't agree on who should go to the wedding.

Then the wife had the idea that they should go and ask the talking mountain who should go to the wedding. The husband asked first, "Should I go to the wedding or should I stay at home?" "Stay at home," replied the mountain. Then the wife asked, "Should I stay at home or should I go to the wedding?" "Go to the wedding," came the reply. "There you are," said the wife, "the mountain agrees with me!" And so she went to the wedding.

Do you know why the mountain agreed with her?

The Cheeky Gosling

"My dear daughter," said Mother Goose, "we've been invited to our relations so don't show me up by being cheeky in front of everyone!" The little gosling promised faithfully to be good and not to be cheeky, and waddled along behind her parents on the way to their relations.

When they arrived it wasn't long before the gosling had forgotten her promise and started to chatter constantly. She said to her Auntie, "Why are your feathers so grey? Haven't you had a good wash lately?" As if that wasn't cheeky enough, she then said to her uncle who was a very proud father, "Your goslings look really skinny and hungry."

Mother Goose was furious with her daughter for being so cheeky. She decided to teach her a lesson once and for all, and so she took a blade of grass and tied it around her daughter's beak. The gosling went to bed feeling very hungry that night and was very ashamed for being so cheeky. She had learnt her lesson and was never so cheeky again.

Who's There

It was December. "Soon it will be Christmas," said Martin's grandfather to his grandson one day. "You'd better be good, or else Father Christmas won't bring you any presents." Martin was very worried when he heard this as he remembered all the naughty things he'd done that year. He'd scribbled on his school desk, trampled on the cabbages and had done lots of other naughty things besides.

On Christmas Eve, Martin heard a noise coming from the stairs. Was it Father Christmas bringing him some presents? He had a peep and saw it was only his grandfather. Martin was very concerned that Father Christmas wouldn't be leaving any presents this year and so he made up his mind to be as good as he possibly could be in the future.

The next morning Martin was very relieved to see that Father Christmas had in fact left him lots of toys and games. Wasn't Martin a lucky boy!

The Boundary Stone

There is a pond where, a long time ago, a ghostly form used to appear at midnight. It was, in fact, the form of an old man who carried a heavy boundary stone on his shoulders.

During his life-time he had moved the stone to make his land larger and his neighbour's smaller, and he was made to suffer for this when he died. No matter who he met during these nights of trudging, no one ever answered him when he asked, "Where shall I put the stone?"

One night, a farmer's boy saw the old man. He said to him sympathetically, "Hello old fellow, can't you find any peace, then?" The old man shook his head and asked, "Where shall I put the stone?" The young boy replied, "Put it back where you found it." With an almighty thrust the old man threw the stone back to where he'd originally found it. The stone landed in its old position and the old man vanished because he had been freed from his curse.

The Fox and the Mouse

One day the fox went up to the mouse and said scornfully, "What a stupid looking, tiny little animal you are!" This annoyed the mouse so he challenged the fox to a race.

The fox got into position and the mouse blew the starting whistle and the race began. The fox was well in the lead at the half-way point and was sure that he would win.

As he approached the finishing line he decided to look round to see exactly how far behind the mouse was. He turned round, but couldn't see the mouse anywhere — and then he heard a little voice coming from behind say, "I'm right behind you, Mr Fox."

The crafty little mouse had ridden all the way on the fox's bushy tail and when the fox had turned round at the end of the race the mouse had jumped down and crossed the finishing line first! The fox felt very ashamed at being beaten by a mouse and never again did he make fun of the mouse for being so small.

A Horse Goes to Town

Sultan is a good natured old horse who's helped lots of children to learn to ride. Day after day, year after year, he has followed the instructor round the paddock and obeyed the rider's instructions.

Then one day when the riding instructor was having his usual midday nap, Sultan seized his opportunity and trotted out of his stable.

Sultan had always yearned for adventure and now he'd got the chance to be free at last! He decided to go to town and it wasn't long before he arrived in the shopping centre. The crowds of people and the noise of the traffic did frighten him a little but, all in all, he rather enjoyed his freedom.

Then, a policeman approached him and said, "You're a danger to the other traffic, since you've no number plate, no lights, no safety belts and no brakes. I'm placing you under arrest." This was all too much for poor old Sultan. He reared and galloped back to the safety of his stable. The instructor was still asleep so he was able to slip back into the comfort of his peaceful life.

Treasure Trove

Barry always spends the Summer holidays at his Aunt Jane's. She has a lovely big house which is surrounded by a garden. Barry loves to go climbing in the trees and to build secret dens in the bushes.

One day, Aunt Jane said to Barry, "I need your help, Barry, to take down the old shed at the bottom of the garden." Barry agreed to help his Aunt dismantle the shed, which had been badly damaged by the wind and was to be replaced with a new one.

First of all, they removed the roof, then the sides, and then they began to hack out the floor with a pick axe. Barry hit something very hard as he was taking up the floor boards and when he dug it out he found a metal box. Excitedly, he prized open the lid with the axe and lots of gold and silver coins and a few papers spilled out.

"Goodness gracious, you've found a real treasure trove," said his Aunt. She read through the documents and then exclaimed, "My father buried this before the last war!"

Since Aunt Jane's father had died such a long time ago she inherited all the treasure. But, of course she didn't forget to reward Barry for finding it. He was very happy when his Aunt gave him a handful of gold and silver coins for discovering the treasure trove.

Mother's Day

Amanda couldn't decide what to get her Mother for Mother's Day. She asked the birds "Would you serenade my mother on Mother's Day?" But the birds just said, "Serenade her yourself."

She then approached a rabbit and said, "Would you do a dance for my mother on Mother's Day?" But the rabbit just shook his head and said, "Do a dance for her yourself."

Amanda then met an old story teller and asked, "Would you tell my mother a story for Mother's Day?" The story teller just laughed and said, "Read her one yourself."

Next Amanda approached the flowers in the meadow and asked, "Would you come and decorate my mother's table on Mother's Day?" The flowers replied, "We'll come gladly, but you must bend down and pick us." Amanda gathered a lovely bunch of flowers and arranged them in a vase.

Amanda not only arranged the flowers, but she sang, did a dance and read her mother a story on Mother's Day.

The Saint Bernard Dog

A hundred years ago, when there weren't as many mountain passes as there are now, several monks lived with their Saint Bernard dogs near a pass high up in the mountains in an isolated monastery.

Whenever a mountaineer got into difficulties and lost his way, especially when deep snow covered the mountains, the Saint Bernard dogs would rescue the hiker from distress. Each dog carried a flask of brandy attached to his collar, so that the freezing hiker could drink from it and so gain warmth and strength.

One night all the dogs were sleeping except for Bernie, who was woken by the sound of a distress call coming from the mountain pass. Instantly he ran out in the direction of the voice. As he raced along, he did not notice that his collar, and with it the flask of brandy, had fallen off.

At last, he reached the exhausted climber who was almost buried in the snow. Bernie

stood in front of the man, as he always did, to offer him the flask of brandy, but then the dog noticed that the flask was not there. How could he warm the man, then? Bernie did the right thing. He snuggled up close to the man to warm him with his thick, soft, furry body. Then he began to bark as loudly as he could to wake the other monks and dogs in the monastery to come and rescue them.

Soon, one of the monks heard Bernie barking and set out with several other dogs and a sleigh. "Well done," said the monk to Bernie, "but where is your brandy flask?" Bernie just gazed adoringly with his soft brown eyes at his master. The climber was helped onto the sleigh and taken to the monastery.

On the way back the monk spotted the flask in the snow. He lifted up both the flask and collar and said, "Your collar is well and truly worn out, Bernie, you certainly deserve a new one right away!"

The Clever Farmer

There was once a clever and cunning farmer who wanted to make a fool of the devil. And this is how he did it.

When the farmer had finished ploughing his fields, the devil appeared before him, sitting on a pile of hot coals. "Are you sitting on some buried treasure?" asked the farmer. "But of course I am," replied the devil, "I'm sitting on the exact spot where there's silver and gold buried." "But the treasure is buried on my land, so it's mine," said the farmer.

"If you give me half of what your fields produce for two years then you can have the treasure because I have enough gold and silver already, but I'd really like some vegetables," suggested the devil. The farmer agreed and declared, "So that there's no argument when it comes to sharing out the vegetables, you can have what's above ground and I'll keep whatever's below ground." The devil agreed to this but he had no idea that the farmer planned to grow turnips.

At harvest time the devil arrived to collect his share. But all he found was yellow leaves whilst the farmer had lots of turnips from below ground. "Next time, don't you dare try to trick me," cried the devil angrily. "Next time, you can have what's above ground and I'll have whatever's below ground," said the devil. "That suits me fine," said the farmer as he'd already planned to grow wheat.

The following year the devil appeared again at harvest time, but he was left with stubble and the farmer had wheat.

The devil was so outraged that he vanished at once and was never seen again. The farmer collected the buried treasure and lived happily for the rest of his days.

The Gigantic Dog

Johnny is a nice little boy but he is forever exaggerating and does not always tell the truth.

At tea one evening, he said, "The new people who've just moved in round the corner have such a gigantic dog, it couldn't fit into this room."

The family were all amazed at this. Johnny went on, "He has such a large mouth he could eat a child in one mouthful." The whole of the family were speechless at this remark, they had never heard of such a big dog before.

"His legs are so strong he could knock a man over with one kick," added Johnny. "Well if that's the case I certainly don't want to meet such a monstrous animal," remarked Johnny's father.

"There's one thing I'd like to know," joined in Johnny's elder brother, "how come there's a normal-size kennel in the garden that is just right for an average size dog?"

Johnny paused for a moment and then said, "Perhaps the people let out some air from the dog in the evening and then pump him up again in the morning so that he can spend the night in the kennel." The whole family burst out laughing when they heard this explanation, which made little Johnny feel rather hurt to say the least! But then he had been making up the story as he went along, and he'd enjoyed shocking his parents and brother.

The Umbrella

A long, long time ago when dwarves and goblins still lived in the woods, there was once a goblin who got caught in a heavy shower of rain whilst berry-picking in the woods. He just managed to shelter under the cover of a toadstool when the rain began to pour down.

Soon the shower began to ease off. "What should I do?" wondered the goblin to himself. "If I take a chance now, it might start to pour down again in a few minutes. However, if I wait much longer it will soon be dark and then I might not even find my way home!"

He put his finger on his nose and thought hard. "I know what," he cried, "I'll carry the toadstool home with me above my head, then it will protect me from the rain!" And that is just what he did. He carried the toadstool in one hand and the basket of berries he had collected that afternoon in the other. He stayed as dry as a bone under the toadstool and soon arrived home.

A magpie had been watching the goblin make his way home and told all the other animals about the goblin and the toadstool.

One day news of this reached the human beings and as a result they invented the umbrella!

Roland's Savings

For his fifth birthday Roland was given a savings book so that once a month he could go to the bank and pay in some money.

Roland didn't really understand about banks. "What does that man behind the counter do?" asked Roland one day. His mother explained that the man put the money into Roland's account so that it would gain interest. "What's interest?" asked Roland.

"It's when the bank lets your money increase so that it's worth more when you draw it out," explained Roland's Mummy.

Roland found this all very confusing and, one day, he decided to find out for himself what really happened to his money. The man behind the counter recognised Roland and asked in a kindly way what he wanted. Roland replied, "I would like to see the money that's in my account," and he handed over his savings book.

The man smiled, counted out the exact amount of money that was stated in the book and showed it to the boy. Roland said, "Thank you, please put it back in the till and let it grow some more!"

The Roundabout Car

It was night-time. The roller coaster, the shooting gallery and the roundabouts were all quite still on the fair ground, but when the clock struck midnight, they all sprang to life. The swings started to swing to and fro and the cars on the roundabout began to chat to one another.

"I'm bored and fed-up," said the little blue car, "sick and tired of going round and round in a circle all day long, I want to do something more exciting." "Be satisfied with what you've got," said the bus. "The outside world is very dangerous indeed."

"That may be, but I'd love to drive down the street just once."

No sooner had the little blue car said this than, as if by magic, it was whisked down from the roundabout and set free to go wherever he chose. The little blue car drove off very quickly to see for itself what the outside world was really like.

It sped along the streets and soon came to the town centre. The car really enjoyed looking at all the lovely things in the shop windows. Then it heard a terrible noise which was getting closer all the time. Then it saw a huge machine coming towards it at a terrible rate, spraying jets of water all over the street, with huge whirling brushes attached to it.

"AAaaaaahhhhh!" screeched the little blue car. It turned round and sped back to the safety of the fairground as fast as it could go.

"I met this dreadful monster that was spraying out jets of water!" said the blue car to its fairground friends, when it was safely back on the roundabout. "That was only a road sweeper!" declared the bus, knowingly.

Then there was silence as the clock struck one, so we will never know what the little blue car said in reply to the bus.

The Birthday Present

"You'll never guess what I got for my birthday," said William to his friend, Andrew.

"Alright," said Andrew, "I bet you that I can guess what you got for your birthday in just three guesses."

"Go on then, guess . . .," said William.

"A camera?" suggested Andrew.

"No, not a camera," replied William.

"A train set, then?" suggested Andrew.

"No, wrong again, you've only one guess left. Think carefully before you say anything. Here's a clue — you can see for a long way, if you have one!" said William to his friend. "I know!" yelled Andrew, "a pair of binoculars!" "Well guessed," said William and showed his friend his new present. They spent the rest of the day looking at the flowers and birds through the new pair of binoculars.

The Proud Princess

There was once a beautiful Princess who was also very proud, so she was known as the Proud Princess. Many Princes came to the palace to offer her their hand in marriage but none of them met with her approval.

Then one day, a handsome man came to the palace who was the son of a magician. He asked the Proud Princess to marry him. But the Princess would not accept, instead she asked him to bring her some presents. First of all, he must give her a gold ring with three rubies. The young man had learnt a lot of magic from his father and he produced a gold ring with three rubies which he gave to the Princess.

The Proud Princess was not satisfied with the ring and she asked for a pair of silver shoes. The magician's son produced these but the Princess was not impressed and did not even thank him for them. So the young man decided to punish her for her ingratitude.

Next, the Proud Princess demanded a crystal palace and a park filled with the rarest creatures of the world. But the young magician was so cross that he turned her into a goose girl and she had to tend a gaggle of geese. He turned her palace into a simple cottage and no Princes ever came to woo her because she was no longer a Princess. And so she stayed a simple goose girl for the rest of her life, because she had been far too proud.

The Young Litter Lout

Carl was a very untidy boy. He was forever leaving a trail of things behind him as he went on his way. His mother was always having to clear up his toys which would be strewn across the bedroom floor and no amount of scoldings would make him put them away.

Out of doors, Carl was just as untidy. He would leave his sweet papers in the front garden and just recently, he had thrown an empty bottle of lemonade into a wood.

He ate a banana on his way to school one morning. Then he threw the skin over his shoulder onto the pavement. Then, someone tapped him on the shoulder and said, "Young man, I think you've forgotten something."

Carl turned round and saw an elderly gentleman holding out the banana skin that he had thrown away. Carl took the banana skin from the man and feeling very ashamed of himself, he put it in a litter bin.

The old man had not scolded him as his mother did every day, but Carl paid more attention to the old man, stopped dropping litter and began to be tidier.

The Disobedient Dwarf

Deep down in the roots of the oak tree lived a dwarf family — Daddy, Mummy and their seven children. The youngest dwarf, Minnie, was the most disobedient and mischievious of them all.

One day, Minnie woke early and decided to go off on an adventure all on her own although that was something her Mummy did not allow. Minnie crept out from the roots and went wandering into the forest.

Soon she got tired of walking aimlessly around and she decided to rest under a tree that was covered in blue berries. Suddenly, an enormous bird swooped down and ate some of the berries off the tree.

"That must be an eagle," thought Minnie to herself. At that moment, one of the berries hit Minnie on the head, burst, and covered her in a blue juice that tasted quite pleasant when she licked it off her fingers. No matter how much she tried to rub the stain off her dress, she just couldn't shift it. What could she do? She decided to go home and face her mother, there was just nothing else she could do.

So she set off for home, feeling quite dismal. She dreaded seeing her mother with her dress in this state.

Minnie need not have worried so much about meeting her family again, because they all roared with laughter when they saw her covered in blue berry juice. Her mother did, however, scold her for going off on her own and warned her not to do it again.

The Pied-Piper

There was once a terrible famine in the town of Hamlin because all the mice and rats had eaten all the food, leaving the people with nothing to eat.

All the people of Hamlin began to panic as well as being very hungry, and longed for a way to get rid of the mice and rats.

Then a minstrel who played a pipe arrived in the town. He promised he could end the famine. The mayor of Hamlin offered him a large reward if he could get rid of the rats.

So the musician picked up his pipe and played a haunting melody. At once all the rats and mice in the town followed the pied-piper as he played the haunting tune. He led the rats and mice out of the town towards the river where they all drowned. So the famine ended and all the people were very happy.

The piper returned to the town to collect his reward, playing a cheerful tune as he walked along. All the children began to follow the piper out of the town but as soon as the mayor paid the piper he stopped playing and the children ran back to their homes.

The Giant's Toy

High up in the mountains lived a giant with his daughter. They lived in a gigantic castle.

One day the giant went down to the lush green valley with his daughter. They took gigantic footsteps all over the meadows.

In a field the giant's daughter noticed a plough between two oxen with a farmer pushing the plough. She bent down and placed the plough and oxen in her apron and took it back to the castle.

Then her giant father asked, "What have you got there?" The daughter replied that she'd found a new toy and showed the plough and oxen to her father.

"No, dear, that's not a toy," said her father severely, "how would we giants survive if there were no hardworking farmers ploughing the fields to grow crops?"

The giant's daughter then realised that the oxen and plough were not a toy and so she returned them to the valley so that the farmer could carry on ploughing the field and growing crops.

An Unusual Ride

Ingrid went to spend her Summer holidays on a farm. She had never been to a farm before, so it was all new to her.

There were so many different kinds of animals on the farm, different types of country smells, different food and strange noises to get used to, but Ingrid soon began to love life in the country. She enjoyed living on the farm so much that she began to help the farmer and his family with their work.

One day, she met the farmer's son who was in charge of the cows. It was very peaceful until Ingrid had an idea. She decided she wanted to ride a cow.

She scrambled up on to one of the cow's backs, and the cow trotted around the field. She was enjoying the bumpy ride very much.

Then suddenly the cow began to do a few little jumps and Ingrid fell off. Luckily she did not hurt herself because she landed in the soft grass. "I'm never going to ride a cow again," said Ingrid to the farmer's boy who replied, "Cows are not for riding, they are for producing milk! Silly girl, you have a lot to learn about life in the country!"

The Orchard

Mr Miller is a friendly old gentleman who lives in an old house with a big orchard. He has the sweetest cherries, the juiciest pears and the reddest apples in his orchard.

So it isn't surprising that Mr Miller has lots of uninvited guests visiting his orchard at harvest time. No, I do not mean just the birds, I am referring here to the local children who love to have a secret harvest of their own at Mr Miller's. They take all his best cherries, pears and apples, leaving Mr Miller with only the rotten fruit.

This Summer Mr Miller put up the following notice at the entrance to his orchard. "To the children who come to take my fruit — please leave me some this year. Also, would they kindly refrain from trampling on the strawberry patch and would they please take care of the rose bushes — signed Mr Miller."

The local children read this notice and felt very guilty and ashamed of themselves for pinching fruit that did not belong to them.

The Inkblot Man

Every day, Ann would call for Helen and they would walk to school together. One morning she did not come so Helen set off on her own.

There was no traffic on the roads today, and Helen did not see any of the other pupils on the way to school. When she reached school, the door was shut, which was odd. Helen found it very hard to push the door open but in the end she succeeded.

The corridors were completely empty. No teachers, prefects or pupils were about. Helen's footsteps echoed as she walked down the long corridor towards her classroom.

The classroom was also empty, but, all the same, Helen sat down at her desk as usual. As she was waiting, she heard a noise coming from the cupboard in the corner. The cupboard door opened and a round, blue, little man appeared. He hopped onto the pile of books on the teacher's desk and started to shout, "I'm the inkblot man, I stain children's books." Then he jumped up and down on a book and made lots of blots on the page.

Then he turned to the next book. Helen recognised it as her own book and called out, "Hey, go away, that's my book." Helen was about to burst into tears but then she woke up and realised it had all been a dream. There was no school today because it was Saturday!

The Fox and the Goose

The fox was out walking one day when he came across a group of geese in a meadow. He said to them, "I'm going to eat you all up, one after the other. You are all sitting there looking so smug, you deserve to be eaten."

The geese were shocked at this and became very flustered. They started flapping about. In the end, one of them plucked up the courage to reply to the fox and said, "If we're all going to die then could we have one last request — please, Mr Fox. Could we say a prayer before you eat us?"

The fox agreed to this request. The geese began to pray, "Gaa, gaa, gaa . . ." they all started to cackle at once and they carried on and on cackling in this way. Every time the fox asked them to stop the geese made the noise louder. After a while the fox couldn't stand it any longer and went away hungry.

The Cunning Ants

Mr Weaver had a beautiful pear tree in his orchard which attracted lots and lots of ants. One day Mr Weaver decided to get rid of the ants. He attached a band of glue around the trunk of the tree which would trap the ants as they made their way up to the pears. Mr Weaver was sure his pears would now be safe from the ants.

It was not long before a party of ants climbed the trunk and reached the band of glue. They tested it carefully with their legs and mouths and realised that it was very sticky and that they would get stuck if they went through it.

So the ants turned round and walked back down the trunk to the ground. Quickly they formed a plan so that they would still be able to get to the pears.

So, one behind the other, each ant carried a grain of sand up the tree trunk and placed it on the glue until a bridge of sand had been made across the band of glue. Then the ants were able to carry on up the tree trunk to reach the juicy, ripe pears quite safely without fear of getting stuck in the glue! Yet again the ants had outwitted poor Mr Weaver.

The Children's Circus

Once upon a time there was a group of children who lived on Broad Street. One day they decided to form a children's circus.

Martina, the eldest would be the Circus Director, Robert would be the clown, Stephen the magician, Tony the artist and Roger the poster maker and ticket seller. They all set to work preparing for the circus.

When the programme was ready, the children had to try and find a huge tent which they could hold the circus in. Where on earth would they find such a tent? Martina decided that they should write to the mayor and ask him if he knew where they could get a tent. The letter went like this — "Dear Mr Mayor, we have formed a children's circus, but we do not have a tent. Please be kind to us and help us find a tent. — lots of love, Martina, Circus Director." Then they posted the letter and a few days later they received a reply.

"Dear Children from Broad Street," began the letter from the Mayor. "You will receive a tent next week. The army often use the type of tent that would be just right for a circus and will gladly lend you one for your circus."

The children jumped for joy when they had all read the letter and they cried, "We've got a tent, we've got a tent!" Roger began to make lots of notices advertising the circus and Stephen practised his tricks to perfect his magician's act.

Meanwhile Martina learnt her introductory speech off by heart and Robert practised putting on his clown's make-up.

On the night of the circus, all the parents and friends came to the tent which the children had put up in a nearby field. Martina made her speech beginning with the words, "Ladies and Gentlemen, welcome, and a special welcome to Mr Mayor . . ."

The Magic Tin

There was once a farmer's wife who was always unlucky. She watched her savings dwindle away and her estate go to ruin.

So one day she went up to a hermit who lived in the woods. She told him of her unfortunate situation. "Nothing ever goes right for me. Can you help me?" she asked. The hermit gave her a small magic tin that was locked and said, "You must take this tin into every room in the house three times each day and then soon you'll find that things will start improving." The farmer's wife thanked him for the tin and said that she would return at the end of one year.

The farmer's wife carried out the hermit's instructions faithfully and carried the tin around with her three times each day into every room. When she did this, she noticed all sorts of things going on that should not be.

For instance, she noticed a farm worker had fallen asleep in the cellar, and the cooker in the kitchen had been allowed to go out. She saw that the stables had not been cleaned out and the horses had not been fed. Each day the farmer's wife noticed more things which needed to be put right.

When the year was up, she returned the tin to the hermit and said, "Thank you very much for the use of the tin, things are going a lot better now. Tell me, what is in the tin that brings such good luck?" The hermit smiled as she asked this and said that there was nothing in the tin. The farmer's wife had created the good luck herself by taking more notice of what was going on at the farm.

The Hunter and the Giant

There was once a hunter who, one day, was going through the wood. He had fastened his gunpowder in a bag around his shoulder. On his way to do some hunting, he met a friendly giant who was known for his stupidity. "Where are you going?" asked the giant. "I'm going hunting," replied the hunter. "What does it look like I'm going to do — do you think I'm going to church dressed like this?"

"What's that around your shoulders?" asked the giant pointing at the bag of gunpowder. "That's filled with tobacco, it's my tobacco pouch," replied the hunter. "Would you like to try some?" The giant put some of the tobacco into his pipe and lit the pipe and began to smoke it. "Ooohh that's horrible! I cannot understand how you manage to smoke that, it's awful!" remarked the giant.

And then the giant went on his way whilst the hunter laughed and laughed at the giant's stupidity.

The Elephant Mouse

Elsa was the middle mouse out of a family of five. One day, she decided that she wanted to be the biggest mouse in the world, in fact she got it into her head that, with a bit of effort, she could become as big as an elephant.

The other mice just laughed at her and thought she was silly to want to put on weight. Everybody else wanted to lose weight. Elsa, however, started to eat like a horse! She was forever in the kitchen nibbling between meals and having third helpings at mealtimes.

She became bigger and fatter with every day that went by. Because she had put on so much weight she could not get into her clothes. But she carried on regardless of what anyone said to her because her aim was to be as big as an elephant.

One day, Daddy Mouse said, "We'll have to move house, because Elsa takes up so much room here that there's not enough room left for the rest of us! This mouse hole is far too small for us now!" All the family agreed, so they started packing for the move.

On the day of the move, Elsa was so fat that she could not squeeze out of the mouse hole. So she had to stay behind, all alone, in the mouse hole without the others. Elsa was so unhappy that she sulked in a corner for hours and hours and then she finally fell asleep. She slept for two weeks and when she woke up she realised that she had lost a lot of weight.

She managed to squeeze out of the mouse hole now that she was much thinner, so she went to join the rest of the family at the new mouse hole. They were all overjoyed to see her again and decided to move back to their old home now that Elsa was back to a normal size! So all the family started packing again, and this time they did it very quickly.

The Cured Patient

There was once a rich man in Holland who did not work, but just spent all his time eating and drinking. In the end he became so fat that he could barely fit through the doorway. He felt very unfit and wrote to a famous Doctor in Amsterdam for some advice on how he should get fit.

The Doctor replied —

"Dear Sir, you really ought to come and see me, not by coach or on horseback but on foot. You must not eat anything on the journey. If you do not obey these instructions, then you will regret it later in life."

The rich man was by now very worried about his unhealthy body, so he decided to carry out the Doctor's advice. He set off by foot for Amsterdam and it took him a fortnight to get there.

When he arrived, he felt fit and well. In fact, he felt better than he had felt for ages. He went to the Doctor and thanked him for this miraculous cure.

The Doctor said to him, "You were eating too much food and not taking enough exercise. By walking here you have cured yourself, because you have worked off all the excess fat." The rich man paid the Doctor for his good advice and went back home feeling very pleased. From that day on, the rich man lived a healthier, more active life.

A Young Rascal

A young boy stood outside the front door of a block of flats and tried in vain to reach one of the bells on the top row. Even when he stood on tiptoes, he still could not reach it.

"May I help you?" asked an old lady. "Yes, if you would not mind," said the young boy. "Could you please ring that bell for me up on the top row, because I am too small to reach it," he said.

She rang the bell and then the little boy said to the old lady, "Now you've got to run away. This is just a game to make the person answer the door when there is no one there!"

The young rascal ran as fast as lightning down the street, leaving the old lady looking totally bewildered. The poor old lady was then left to explain the whole story to the person who came to answer the door. They were both very cross with the little boy!

The Apprentice

Max, the dwarf had been Rosa, the witch's apprentice for a long time now. He had watched her mixing the herbs, concocting healing potions. He helped her wherever he could in collecting the berries and plants which are used in the magic potions. He had really enjoyed his time with Rosa, but he longed to be allowed to cast spells and make up the magic potions himself.

Rosa was very good to Max and only once was she angry with him and that was when he used her broom to sweep the kitchen floor. She snatched the broom from him and said, "Don't touch that broom again, it's only to be used by a real witch to fly to a witches' dance." Then she gave Max a normal broom to sweep the kitchen floor. It was not Max's fault because he had no idea that a witch's broom was so special! So he carried on with his household chores.

One day, Rosa said to Max that it was time he learnt all the witch's spells off by heart. Max was very excited about learning all the spells but he didn't realise just how much work there would be in learning them.

The next day Rosa handed Max her huge book of spells. He found this very difficult to understand but plodded on, as he really wanted to cast spells and be a witch.

Rosa was very strict with him and made sure he learnt the spells properly. One day Rosa was satisfied that the young apprentice had learnt the spells and could now begin to master witchcraft. But that is another story.

Chasing Birds

There was once a kitten called Kitty who was young and playful and had not yet experienced hunting or catching mice and birds.

One day, she was lying quite contentedly on the sofa dozing, when she suddenly heard the sound of a bird singing. Kitty woke up and looking through the window saw a Great Titmouse sitting on a branch of a fir tree.

Kitty leapt up and jumped towards the bird! Pow! Kitty hit the windowpane and fell to the ground. At first she did not move to get up, and then she stood up again and returned to the comfort of the sofa. She felt really ashamed of herself.

All for a Pound

A well-dressed young man once went into a restaurant, sat down at a table, and said to the landlord, "Can I get a good meal here for my money?" "Of course you can," replied the landlord.

So the young man ordered soup, meat, vegetables and potatoes, and a dessert and said, "I'll have all that for my money." The landlord hurried to get his meal.

When the young man had eaten his three course meal he went to pay at the counter. He gave a one pound coin to the landlord, and said, "There you are, my money for the meal." The landlord was taken aback and said, "But sir, the meal cost much more than one pound."

The young man replied, "I said I wanted a meal for my money and that's all my money," he said pointing at the one pound coin. "You've really caught me out with such a clever trick," said the landlord, "I'll give you five pounds, if you go and do the same thing at the restaurant up the road."

The young man put the five pounds into his pocket and as he went out of the door, he said, "The restaurant up the road sent me here!" With that last comment, the young man hurried out of the restaurant. The landlord was not angry for long because he had such a good sense of humour.

The Old Car

There was an old car at the edge of a wood which was completely crushed and very rusty. What's more it had no tyres or windows.

One day, Matthew and his friends discovered it and from then on they played in it every day. They would sit themselves behind the steering wheel and go for pretend rides along stony streets, making screeching noises as they went round corners.

The forester thought differently. He was disgusted that people should litter the forest with junk, and joined up with a group to remove all the rubbish that had been dumped in the woods. This group was known as 'Action, Wood Clear-up'.

And one day when Matthew and his friends came to play in the old car, it was no longer there. It had been taken away by the 'Action, Wood Clear-up', group.

The boys were very upset that they could not play in the car anymore. "There are lots more old cars dumped, we'll just have to look around a bit until we find another one to play in," said Matthew. What a pity that what Matthew said is true!

On the Beach

Mark was going to spend his first day at the seaside. His mother and father promised to take him for the day. There was great excitement before they left home because Mummy was packing up a picnic.

They set off and Mark just couldn't wait to get there. "Will we be there soon, Mummy," he asked. "When will we be there, Daddy?" he pleaded. Then his Daddy said, "Here we are, Mark, at the sea."

The little boy couldn't believe his eyes, it was so big and the waves kept coming in and going out all the time. "Where do the waves go, Daddy?" he asked.

When they had unpacked the car and carried all the bits and pieces down on to the beach, everyone was feeling quite hungry. They had their lunch, and then the biggest treat — Mark's Daddy said, "I'm going to build a sandcastle, Mark. Do you want to help me?" They built the biggest and best sandcastle on the beach.

All too soon it was time to pack up and go home, but what a wonderful day Mark had had on the beach.

Ketchup Peter

Peter liked to put tomato ketchup on every meal. He adored tomato ketchup more than anything else in the world! His mother said to him one day, "Tell me, doesn't everything taste the same when you put ketchup on it?"

"Oh, you don't understand, Mummy," replied Peter, covering his lamb chop with a large dollop of ketchup. Once, when there was no ketchup left, Peter went right off his food and claimed that everything tasted horrid without it.

Peter hated liver. He would much rather eat just potatoes than liver! His mother had an idea one day. She decided to disguise a piece of liver in bread crumbs to look like a piece of chicken, and when Peter covered it in ketchup he would eat it up greedily not realising he had eaten liver!

Sure enough, Peter put a big dollop of tomato ketchup onto the chicken and gobbled it up greedily. It was only when his mother told him that he had in fact eaten liver, but hadn't been able to taste it because he had covered it in ketchup, that he believed he had eaten it. Peter was taken aback at this. Since then he has tried his best to eat his meals without quite so much tomato ketchup, so that he can actually taste the food!

Keith's Birthday

It is Keith's fifth birthday in three days time. "I'd like to be allowed to stay up very late as a birthday treat," Keith said to his parents. His mother said, "Alright then, you can stay up as long as you like on your birthday."

The day of his birthday arrived and Keith celebrated all day long. He received lots of lovely presents, had a birthday cake with five candles and played lots of party games with his two elder sisters.

When it was evening, Keith's mother told his sisters that it was bedtime, but that Keith was allowed to stay up longer as a birthday treat.

Keith really enjoyed staying up late. He played with his new toys and chatted to his parents. Then his father read the newspaper and his mother did some knitting. When the clock struck ten his parents went up to bed.

He read his book, watched a little more television and then he became very tired and bored staying up on his own. He went running to his parents' room to ask them if he could go to bed now. They replied, "Go to bed whenever you like. But don't forget to turn out all the lights."

So Keith turned out the lights and went to bed. He now realised that staying up late was not much fun after all. In fact he preferred to go to bed at his normal time, and never asked to stay up late again.

The Vineyard

There was once a vineyard owner who knew that he was going to die soon, so he called his two sons to his bed and said to them, "There is some treasure in the vineyard which I leave to you both."

Then he died before the sons had time to ask where the treasure was to be found. A few days went by and the sons started digging in the vineyard for the treasure. They dug up the whole vineyard but they did not find any.

In the end, the elder son said to his brother, "I'm going out into the world to seek my fortune, there's no treasure to be found here." Then he said goodbye and left.

The younger son cultivated the vineyard, and after a year, he gazed in astonishment at the vines — each one carried three times as many grapes as the previous year. At last he understood his father's dying words. Digging up the vineyard had made the treasure — the good harvest.

So the young farmer dug the vineyard and harvested a greater treasure each year and soon grew the finest grapes for miles around!

Tina and the Mushroom

One beautiful Autumn day, Tina went with her mother and her sister, Anita into the wood to collect mushrooms. It had rained the day before and lots of mushrooms had popped up out of the earth. Their mother gave them a basket each and they went off to see who could get the most mushrooms.

"Hurrah! I've found an enormous mushroom. Look here everyone!" cried Tina. Her mother replied, "I've found lots of tiny mushrooms!" Only little Anita hadn't had any luck, and then she suddenly saw an enormous red and white spotted mushroom.

"Look what I've found!" she called out excitedly. Her mother replied, "For goodness sake, that's a poisonous toadstool, throw it away at once!" "But it's so pretty!" said Anita sulkily. "Just because it looks nice doesn't mean to say that it's good for you. We are only collecting mushrooms that are in this book. All the others we leave alone," said her mother, showing Anita the book. They looked in the book for the red and white spotted mushroom, but it was not there which meant that it was poisonous.

Rose Oversleeps

Rose overslept one morning. She did not hear the alarm go off, and so, when she finally woke up she had to rush around to get ready for school in time.

She raced into the bathroom for a quick wash. She was so hasty that she splashed water all over herself and even dropped the toothpaste on the floor. She then hurried to get dressed and, as she was rushing so much, she put her jumper on back to front and put on odd socks! She jammed the zip as she tried to fasten her skirt, and a button came off her blouse.

When she finally got down to breakfast her mother could not believe her eyes for her daughter looked as if she had just crawled through a hedge backwards! She had also forgotten to comb her hair and it looked like a haystack. Rose had to rush back up to her bedroom to comb her tangled locks.

She gulped down her breakfast and then was about to set off for school when she noticed she had put her shoes on the wrong feet. "What a morning!" exclaimed Rose to her mother. "You'd do better if you remembered the saying — Less haste, more speed!" replied her mother laughing.

There was once a young fawn who was very curious. His mother worried a lot because he was so nosy and she felt sure it would lead him into trouble.

One day, when the fawn's family were having their midday nap, he decided to go for a walk in the woods. If the fawn's mother knew she would not let him go alone into the woods, so he crept off quietly without waking anyone.

The fawn wandered around nibbling at the bushes as he went, until finally he came across a bush that he had never seen before — one with red flowers which smelt so sweet he just had to try it! But to his surprise the flower tasted very bitter. He was disappointed, but decided to eat the stalk.

Then the fawn crept back to his family. He lay down alongside his mother as if he had been there all the time.

It was not long before he felt very ill. The young fawn groaned and groaned and woke the rest of the family.

"What is the matter?" asked his mother concerned. "I've got the most awful stomach ache," said the fawn. "I don't understand it, we've all been eating the same grass," replied the mother.

So the silly fawn had to tell how he had crept off and eaten a strange flower.

"Tell me what this flower looked like," said the mother. The fawn told her about the red flower and the mother shouted, "Oh dear, that was a daphne, a very poisonous plant — you should never eat that plant."

Because he had eaten only one flower the fawn did not die, he just had to suffer terrible stomach ache for a day or two. From then on he stayed close to his mother and never wandered off alone again.

Weather Predicting

The farmer wanted to bring in the hay but he was not sure whether it would be a sunny day or not. So, first he asked the frog what the weather would be like the next day.

"Tell me, Mr Frog, will it rain tomorrow?" asked the farmer. "Croak, croak, I'm afraid I can't tell you, you must go and ask the old rooster."

The farmer then went up to the rooster and asked, "Tell me Mr Rooster, will it rain tomorrow?" The rooster replied, "Cockadoodle do, I can't tell you, you'll have to decide for yourself."

So the farmer walked home slowly and wondered what the weather would be like the next day. When he got home, his wife turned to greet him and said, "The swallows are flying so high in the sky that it will probably rain tomorrow. I know it's an old wives tale, but I always go by the swallows." The farmer took her word for it and decided not to bring in the hay the next day after all.

Perhaps that's where the saying, 'Make hay while the sun shines' comes from.

The Weather Spirits

Whenever human beings complain about the bitterly cold weather in Autumn, the three weather spirits always feel pleased with themselves. These spirits are the Rain Man, the Cloud Lady and the Autumn Wind. They enjoy Autumn more than any of the other seasons.

They have all met up for a chat today. "Isn't it a wonderful time," said the small, grey Rain Man, "I make huge puddles and I enjoy sending heavy showers of rain — it is great fun!"

"Yes indeed," said the Cloud Lady. "I love to go along meadows and fields, shrouding everything in thick, grey cloud which really annoys all the human beings!"

"I love to blow and whistle as loud as I can," added the Autumn Wind. "I especially enjoy playing with the leaves and making them dance! Oh, yes! Autumn is the best time of all!"

The three of them carried on chatting together for a long while. "What a pity that human beings do not like us as much as the Sun," they all said. Then they went their separate ways to make more cold Autumn weather.

Rosa and the Dwarf

One day, when the witch, Rosa, was going through the forest collecting herbs she suddenly heard a whimpering noise coming from nearby. She looked behind her and saw a grubby, little man wearing a moss green hat, at the foot of a gigantic fir tree.

The dwarf had fallen over a root and hurt his foot. Rosa hurried to help him, and said to him, "Come with me, to my house and I'll put some special cream on your sore foot." And so she helped the little man to stand up and gave him a piggy-back to her house. The clever witch soon mended the sore foot.

The little man stood up, raised his little green hat and said, "Thank you kindly, good witch, I shall never forget this."

The little man and the witch got on very well together and Rosa invited the little dwarf, whose name is Max, to stay with her to learn the art of witchcraft. Max jumped at this chance and decided to stay and learn to cast spells, because he had always wanted to be a witch.

Max's First Lesson

The next day Rosa said to Max, "You've been studying the book of spells for long enough now, let's see you put what you've learnt into practice." Max was very excited at the thought of casting spells for the very first time on his own.

"We'll begin with an easy one first," said Rosa. Max pondered over which one to begin with and when he had finally made up his mind, he said, "Crows feet and spiders webs, open the door!" And hey presto, the door opened. "Not bad at all for your first go," said Rosa. "Now let's try a harder one. Command fire, to light my hearth to heat up my dinner!"

Max scratched his ear and then he said, "Flies and crows, fire, fire, light the oven where the witch's pans are!" The fire lit up and then went out again. "You blinked whilst you cast the spell, that's why it hasn't worked," scolded the witch, and then she said in a more kindly way, "That happens to the best witches from time to time, especially when learning to cast spells. We'll try again tomorrow as you've done quite enough for one day!" Max agreed with Rosa and was very glad to have a rest because all this magic had made him very tired indeed.

Spring Preparations

When it is Spring, Clive the Gnome Artist has lots to do.

When the big Spring Festival takes place every flower, even the very tiny ones, wants to have the prettiest dress to wear to the Spring Ball. So Clive Gnome is kept very busy mixing lots of different colours. He fills many pots with paint and cleans all his brushes.

Then he loads all these into his little van and drives off into the woods and meadows to paint the flowers. He paints the primroses yellow, and the daisies white and yellow. Then he paints the tulips red and yellow. The bluebells always have to wait until last to be painted bright blue, but they don't mind because they always look so lovely when Clive has finished painting them.

Whilst Clive Gnome is working, he attracts a crowd of admirers; ants, snails, ladybirds and beetles who all look on. Then evening draws in and the hard-working flower painter puts down his brushes and returns home, feeling very tired from his day's work. All the flowers thank him for their beautiful new colours and he is happy knowing that he has done a good day's work. He even gives the grass an extra lick of paint to freshen it, and adds a new tint of green to each tree, ready for the Spring Ball.

The Big Cabbage

Once there were two tradesmen walking through the countryside; Martin, the greengrocer and Simon, the coppersmith. When they passed through a field of cabbages, Simon said, "Look at those big cabbages!"

Martin, who was rather big-headed said scornfully, "What! you call those large? I've been around the world and I've seen a cabbage that was as large as a house!"

"Good heavens," said Simon, "I've also been around the world and I've seen a saucepan that was as large as a church tower." Then Martin looked at him puzzled and asked, "Well, why ever did they need such a large saucepan?"

"To cook your cabbage in!" replied Simon calmly.

The Sun and the Wind

One day, the sun and the wind had a terrible argument as to who was the strongest.

"I can blow so strongly that I can knock off the heads of flowers," boasted the wind.

"On the other hand, I can shine so warmly that ice melts," retorted the sun. And so it went on, until a wise old owl interrupted them. "I've got a suggestion to put to you two," said the owl. "You see that traveller over there, well which ever one of you can make him take his coat off is the strongest and is the winner of this argument."

At once the wind began to blow strongly. The wind even summoned the rain and hail to help. The traveller shivered with cold and pulled his coat tighter around him to keep warm.

Then it was the sun's turn. She sent her warmest rays down to the earth. The ground became dry and the sky turned a deep blue. The traveller felt this warmth and took off his coat. Then he lay down in the shade of an oak tree.

"The sun is the winner," declared the owl. With that, the wind went away and swore never to get into an argument with the sun again.

The Seahorses

Bruno was sitting contentedly on the sea bed chatting to his friend Frederick, who had come to visit him. Frederick was a restless sort of fellow. He had a changeable mind and from time to time he would get the urge to wander and he would swim far away to learn more about the world. He had seen lots of animals on dry land, he was very well travelled for a sea-horse.

Today, however, Bruno could show his friend something new. He leaned back against a piece of coral and showed Frederick all the children he carried around in his pocket. "I keep the kids by me whilst my wife goes off for a swim, and I make sure they eat regularly," explained Bruno to his friend. "Isn't this a marvellous life?" asked Bruno.

His friend had to agree with him. He'd heard that their distant relatives the horses, had to work hard pulling ploughs and taking people for rides. "Just imagine," said Frederick, "men sit on horses and are carried around by them, just because they are too lazy to walk. Some horses even have to pull

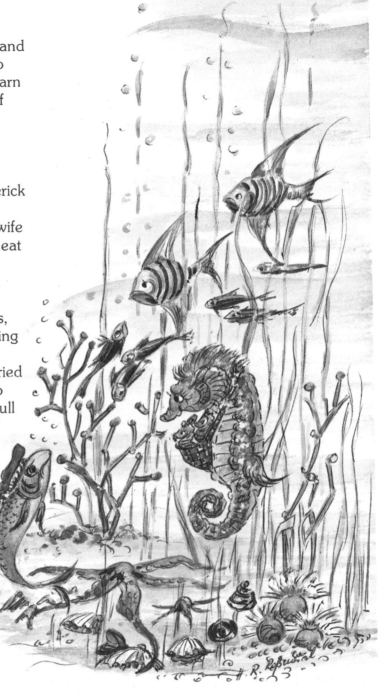

carriages. You're quite right, we sea-horses have a much easier life. Personally, though, I wouldn't like to look after children just yet; I'm off on my travels again now!"

And with that Frederick swam off, leaving Bruno to bring up his children. "Hopefully, none of my children will be as restless as Frederick!" thought Bruno to himself.

The Lazy Kangaroo

There are many kangaroos in Australia and this story is about one of them. There was once a baby boy kangaroo who was carried around in his mother's pouch all the time, and she gave him lots of food and water. The baby kangaroo enjoyed this life very much, but became very lazy because everything was done for him.

Then one day when he'd grown quite big, his mother said to him, "My little one, it's time you came out of the pouch and learned to jump. You must also learn to find food and look after yourself." The young kangaroo didn't want to jump out of the pouch and each time his mother suggested it, he would have yet another feeble excuse to stay in the pouch. "I'm too tired today," or, "It's too cold today," were his favourite excuses.

Then one day a neighbour came to see the mother kangaroo and said, "Your young boy is quite big now, you can't possibly carry him around with you any more. He must be so heavy. Why is he still in the pouch?" "Oh that's a sad story, I'm afraid, my boy is not very well, he has such weak legs that he can't jump, he will probably have to stay in the pouch for the rest of his life," explained Mother kangaroo.

"What's that?" yelled the young kangaroo. "What did you say? — that I'm weak and that I'll never jump? I'll show you how well I can jump." And with that he leapt out of the pouch and jumped around. "At long last," sighed his mother, smiling to herself.

The Bad Apple

"Great!" called Casper to his friend, Sam, "Granny has sent us some apples. Would you like one?" Of course Sam wanted one, since he was always hungry. He bit into the apple and then spat it out — "Yuck!" he cried, "There's a worm in this one."

Casper tried to calm his friend down by saying, "Don't make such a fuss, it'd be far worse if you found half a worm in your apple!" "Half a worm?" said Sam and then he understood his friend's joke, because in that case he'd have eaten the other half of the worm! It wasn't so bad after all!

The Proud Cat

There was once a cat who, quite by chance found an old mirror and decided to take a good look at himself.

It was quite clear that he was more handsome by far than all the other cats in the world. From then on, he decided to walk around on two legs rather than on all fours, so that everyone would see how handsome and elegant he was.

One day, he went to the cobbler's and ordered a pair of very smart boots. He also ordered a flamboyant green hat with a long feather. He was even more proud of his appearance in these new clothes, but then he felt very hungry.

He spotted a mouse and tried to catch it, but his boots hampered him, and try as he might, he just could not catch the mouse. He stumbled over his boots and landed flat on his face. Then, in a rage he tore off his fine boots, threw the hat away and decided to act and look like a normal cat once again.

Stewed Rhubarb

Andrew's best friend was his Daddy. He copied everything his father did, talked like him, and pottered about like him.

A little while ago Andrew helped his father weed the garden. Andrew's father pulled a massive weed out of the ground and said, "Rhubarb, ugh a horrible fruit!" "Ugh rhubarb!" said Andrew too, copying his Daddy, even though he had never eaten or seen rhubarb in his life before.

A little later Andrew went to tea at his Grandma's. His Grandma had made a special meal for him and for pudding there was delicious stewed fruit. Andrew ate it all up and said, "Ooh Granny that was yummy!" "Yes," said Andrew's Grandma, "my stewed rhubarb is famous for being so good."

"Ugh rhubarb!" replied Andrew, and then laughed as he heard himself repeating his father's words. From then on stewed rhubarb became his favourite pudding, and he thought more carefully before he spoke.

Bilberrying

The sun was just going down at the end of a hot July day. In the wood, a little girl and her brother were still hard at work collecting bilberries.

They were the children of a poor family. So they did not want to go home with empty baskets, because their mother needed the bilberries to make a pie. The more they looked and searched for bilberries, the fewer they found, or so it seemed. Disappointed and exhausted they sat down in the soft grass to rest for a moment.

Then the little girl caught a glimpse of a very well-laden branch of bilberries. "Look over there!" she called to her brother, pointing to the bilberries. "Quick, let's go and fill our baskets with those berries, then we can go home and Mummy will be pleased with us."

As they were picking the berries they heard a faint voice saying, "Dear children, please

don't pick me." The two children were amazed when they saw a beautiful bilberry with a crown on her head, in the middle of the branch.

"Don't be afraid, we will not harm you, but please tell us who you are," said the little girl. "I'm Queen of the Bilberries. I'm the only one that stays on this branch year after year to ensure that new berries grow. Do you understand now why I begged you to save my life?" explained the Bilberry Queen.

Then the children stepped back as they saw all the berries hop off the branch and into their baskets. The Queen said, "This is your reward for saving my life." The children clapped their hands and replied, "Thank you, Queen of the Bilberries!" Then they made their way home. They would be able to give their mother the bilberries after all, and she would be able to make a delicious pie. And what a story they would have to tell her.

The Two Brothers

A shopkeeper once had two helpers, John and David, who were brothers. At first they both received the same wage for the work they did, and so things went well for a while.

Then one day, John noticed that his brother was being paid more. So he went up to the shopkeeper and said, "Mr Shopkeeper, you're paying my brother more than me and I want to know why."

"I'll explain why in a minute, first of all go over to the market and see if there are any new potatoes," replied the shopkeeper. So John went over to the market and reported back to the shopkeeper, "Yes, there are new potatoes on the market," he said. "Good," replied the shopkeeper. "Now go and ask what they cost per kilo."

John went back to the market, returned to the shop and said, "The farmer is asking 50p a kilo." "Good," replied the shopkeeper. "Now go and find out how many kilos he can supply me with today."

So John went to the market again, for the third time that morning and came back with the following answer, "The farmer says he can supply you with five kilos today." "Very well, now sit here for a minute," said the shopkeeper.

He then told David to go to the market to see if there were any new potatoes. David came back quickly and said, "There are plenty of new potatoes on the market today. They cost 50p per kilo and you can have five kilos today." Then the shopkeeper turned to John and asked, "Do you understand now why I pay your brother more?"

The New Shoes

Marion went shopping with her mother to buy a pair of new shoes. It was very cold as it was late Autumn and the time for wearing sandals was over. Marion's old boots have become too small for her and she has no suitable shoes to wear during the coming Winter.

She especially enjoyed shopping for shoes and in particular being served by a grown-up. She chose a pair of leather boots with zip fasteners. She tried them on and said, "They pinch a bit on the toes, but they're just the right size otherwise." The sales assistant replied, "It takes a few days before new boots are worn in — they always pinch a bit for the first fortnight or so."

"Then I'll leave them in the cupboard for a fortnight before I put them on," said Marion to the assistant, and she was very puzzled when her mother and the assistant burst out laughing. Do you know why they laughed?

On the Farm

It is early morning on the farm. The squealing piglets are waiting for their breakfast. The cows are mooing in the stable for some hay. The hens are clucking whilst waiting for the corn. The dog is waiting expectantly for his breakfast and the doves are cooing on the roof awaiting their breakfast, too. The little girl runs across the farmyard asking, "Where's my breakfast?"

Only the cat is not hungry. It caught a mouse in the night and has eaten it for breakfast, and now it looks for a warm place to snooze the day away.

The Boiled Eggs

It is Sunday. Daddy, Mummy and the children, Ben and Lucy, are about to have their breakfast. Today, Judy the youngest has prepared the breakfast all by herself. She has set the table, cut the bread, brewed a pot of tea and even boiled the eggs.

Then Judy serves the eggs, the tea and the bread and butter to the rest of the family. They all tuck in straight away because they are very hungry since they had been out for an early morning jog, and had worked up a healthy appetite.

"Well done Judy," her brother and sister called out and clapped as she served the breakfast. "Next time you can make us a real English breakfast of bacon, eggs and sausages — you'd make ever such a good cook," they all praise.

Judy blushes a little as she's not used to such praise from her brother and sister.

The Enraged Wind

There was a terrible storm one evening. There was thunder and lightning and the rain poured down in torrents. The wind found this weather most disagreeable and tried to seek shelter in an old farm house.

First of all, it pushed against the front door, but the door remained firmly closed. Then the wind whistled through the key hole but still could not persuade the door to open. So it blew as hard as it could at the windows. Then it tried climbing on the roof and rattling the tiles, and finally it blew down the chimney.

As it could not get into the house, the wind blew out the stove so that the farmer's wife had soot blown in her face. This is how the wind took its revenge. Then, feeling happier, it went on its way to try its luck elsewhere.

The Little Bird

One day Peter went with his father along the path that led through the field. Suddenly, they saw a tiny little bird lying beneath a tree. Peter went up to it to get a closer look and realised that it was dead. "This often happens when a baby bird tries to fly before it has grown its wings," said Peter's father.

Later that same day Peter's father heard a loud shout coming from the front of the house. He hurried outside to see what had happened. He saw that Peter had been trying to ride the big bicycle but he had fallen off and was crying on the ground.

"You remind me of the little bird," said Peter's father. "You, too, want to fly before you have grown wings." Peter nodded in agreement, for although he knew he would never grow wings, he understood his father's remark.

The Sticky Toothbrush

"Where on earth is my toothbrush?" asked George's mother whilst searching the bathroom. "I know where it is," said George and then disappeared.

Soon after he returned with the toothbrush in his hand. Whilst George's mother brushed her teeth, she said in a worried voice, "What's the matter with this brush, I can't get my teeth apart, my jaws are stuck together!"

"Oh, didn't you know," said George sheepishly, "I used your toothbrush to glue my boat back together. It must still be covered in glue!" With that George rushed out of the bathroom, chased by his mother who was waving the toothbrush at him angrily.

The Tired Flower

Jill is a little girl who loves all the animals, all the plants and all the flowers in the world. Whenever she sees an animal suffering, she is filled with compassion for it. And sometimes she even takes a wingless bird home with her, or a damaged butterfly or an injured ladybird.

Yesterday, she found a withered daisy, that a child had obviously picked and then thrown down. She felt sorry for the flower and wanted it to recover. So she took it home with her and planted it in a flower pot with good soil so that it would bloom again. Jill watered the plant and then waited for the wilted stem and leaves to recover.

"It won't grow again," said Jill's mother, "because it needs to have roots to grow and it hasn't got any because it was picked, so it will die." Jill was very upset at this and wondered why flowers needed roots to grow. Aren't sun, water and good earth sufficient for the plant to grow?

New Year's Eve

Last New Year's Eve the four musicians of Bremen, the donkey, the dog, the cat and the cockerel, who had been made into a bronze statue, next to the Bremen Town Hall, suddenly came to life.

At midnight, the cockerel climbed down from the cat, the cat from the dog and the dog from the donkey. The donkey heaved a great sigh of relief and said, "Oh it does feel good not to have to take the weight of you three! Tell me what shall we do now?"

The three animals crowed, miaowed, and barked so loudly that no one could hear themselves speak. "Quietly!" yelled the donkey. "One after the other. First the dog, what do you suggest?" "I'd like to go through the streets and alleys to look for bones in the dustbins," said the dog. "And I," said the cat, "I would like to go to the harbour and eat up the left-over fish." "I'd like to find a farmyard and then I'd be able to crow to my heart's content, even at midnight," said the cockerel.

Last of all the donkey said, "I'd like to wander through the streets and admire myself in the reflection of the shop windows." So the four of them decided to go their separate ways. "Don't forget though," said the donkey, "to be back here at one o'clock because we have to be back on our pedestal by then." The other three agreed to this and went on their way, remembering that they must be back by one o'clock.

I expect you're interested to know how the story of the Bremen musicians turned out. Well, this is what happened.

Shortly before one o'clock the donkey arrived back at the Town Hall, followed by the dog and cat. But where was the cockerel? It was time to climb back onto the pedestal! The donkey looked up and down the street for the cockerel but could not see it anywhere.

Then it came flapping towards him gasping for breath. "You've no idea what happened to me!" shouted the cock excitedly. "I almost ended up in a frying pan because some silly man complained about my crowing! Just imagine, the famous rooster of Bremen in a frying pan!"

"Oh shut up," said the donkey impatiently. "We must climb back on our pedestal at once. We are late enough as it is." At that precise moment the clock struck one. "Quick," said the donkey to the other three, "up onto my back now."

The animals leapt back into position, one on top of the other. "Are you mad?" yelled the donkey at the cat. "Since when has the cat stood beneath the dog? Change places quickly now." The animals changed places, but now the cat was on the top instead of the cockerel. "Swap places you two," yelled the donkey to the cat and cockerel.

At last, just as the clock had chimed one, the animals were in their usual places on the statue. It's a good job too, otherwise whatever would the people of Bremen, and in particular the children, have thought if their favourite musicians were in the wrong places? They certainly would never guess that they had left the statue to go into the town.

The "Don't Know" Ghost

Do you know of the ghost who is forever creating trouble and leaving his traces behind? Of course, this ghost is invisible as are all ghosts, but it does have a name — it is called "Don't know"!

Who left the cellar door open? "Don't know," comes the reply. Who smeared glue all over the chair? — "Don't know," is the answer. Who's trampled over all the flower beds? — Of course the answer is, "Don't know."

Who's hidden the bunch of keys — needless to say the answer is "Don't know"! Oh, if only I could catch this trouble-maker of a ghost! I wonder where I might find him?

At This Moment In Time

It is evening and the Smith family are sitting at the table, having their tea. Then Michael said, "I say Daddy, have you ever thought what might be happening at this moment in time somewhere else in the world?" Michael is just seven and does a lot of thinking about the world.

His father said, "In other parts of the world people are probably having their tea, just like we are." "Perhaps somewhere in Africa a young boy is being told off," mused Michael. "Or an eskimo may be whizzing along on his sleigh in Alaska," said William, Michael's older brother.

All at once the whole family thought about what might be happening in other parts of the world. There was probably a car chase taking place in France; in Ireland a young boy might be flying his kite and in China a young girl might be weaving a basket. . . . "Isn't it wonderful to think what might be happening at this moment in time," said Michael, deep in thought.

Then Michael's mother called out, "At this moment in time, your tea is going cold, so come on, stop thinking so much and eat up or you won't get any pudding." Then she smiled lovingly at her small son who thought so much about the world.

Marsha and the Snakes

Marsha was a poor, little orphan girl who lived in India. One day a conjurer came to the orphanage where she lived and paid a few rupees to take her away with him. From then on it would be Marsha's job to carry the basket containing two snakes, from market place to market place.

Marsha did this for quite some time. Whenever spectators gathered round to watch the conjurer, he would kneel down and play his flute. Then the snakes would push up the lid of the basket and sway in time to the music. At that point Marsha had to walk around the crowd holding out a plate so spectators could give money if they wished. Marsha would then hand all the rupees to the wicked conjurer.

As soon as the conjurer had collected several rupees he would head off for the nearest bar to get drunk, leaving Marsha and the snakes feeling very hungry.

Sometimes sympathetic passers-by would give Marsha a piece of bread or some milk when they saw how under-nourished she looked. Marsha would always share whatever she was given with the two snakes, who had now become her closest friends.

Then one day when she shared her milk with the two snakes, she suddenly heard strange music and everything around her was bathed in a bright light. Marsha looked around in astonishment and then she saw that she was in a splendid palace.

Before her stood a young man and woman dressed in very fine clothes. They looked at Marsha in a friendly way and said, "Your kindness and compassion have freed us from being snakes. You are to stay with us from now on, and we shall treat you as if you were our own child." Marsha was overjoyed and lived happily with the young couple for many years.

Bertha Bumble-bee

When the sun was high in the sky at midday, she decided to have a rest. She flew to her favourite flower, the tulip, and went to sleep in the petals. She dreamt in her sleep, and wondered why bees could not sing like the larks or blackbirds. The only tune the bees knew was — buzz, buzz, buzz. . . .

She wondered whether the old legend was true that the old man had told her about how bees never sang but only buzzed. The legend went like this: There was once a cannibal who sent all insects with a sting out into the world and ordered them to sting all living creatures. He wanted to find out which flesh tasted the best. The bumble-bee had flown a long way and stung many different animals and then one day it stung a human being and the human being screamed out in pain. This scream frightened the bumble-bee.

When the bee reported back to the cannibal all it would say about human flesh was "buzzz, buzzz . . ." because it had had such a shock it could no longer speak, let alone sing.

Since then all bumble-bees have only ever buzzed. They live a peaceful life making honey, buzzing from flower to flower.

The petals of the flowers had only just opened up in the morning sunshine when Bertha Bumble-bee buzzed from flower to flower, collecting pollen and nectar to take back to the hive to make honey. She spent the whole morning doing this, and returned to the hive several times that morning.

The Vain Scarecrow

There was a scarecrow in the middle of the corn field that was so ugly it scared off all the birds. It was dressed in a battered old straw hat, a ripped blanket and a tatty blouse over its thin arms.

It stood alone in the field, sad, because no mouse or bird would talk to him. "It's because I'm so ugly!" said the scarecrow to itself. And when it just could not stand the loneliness any longer, it decided to run away from the field and go into the town.

It was a moonlit night when the scarecrow finally ran away. When it arrived in town it saw some beautiful clothes in a shop window that it longed to have. Then the clock struck midnight and the scarecrow was able to make its dream come true, because midnight is a magic time when wishes sometimes come true. The scarecrow chose a flowered silk dress with a matching hat, white gloves and elegant shoes. Overjoyed with its lovely new clothes, it returned to the field and went to sleep feeling much happier than it had for a long time.

The next morning the scarecrow woke up to find crowds of visitors around it. The birds and mice had come to admire its clothes and to pay it compliments. The scarecrow was overjoyed at having so many friends at long last. The farmer, on the other hand, saw that the scarecrow was not carrying out its job very well and said, "That scarecrow is no good now, I might as well burn it."

Luckily, the wind heard these words and decided to save the scarecrow from this dreadful fate. He blew so hard that the scarecrow's clothes were ripped to shreds and the fine hat was crumpled. He sent a few rain clouds over to the scarecrow. These made it rain so hard that the scarecrow now looked so dishevelled and ugly once again, that all the birds were scared to come near it and kept well away from the corn field.

This satisfied the farmer. The scarecrow remained alone in the middle of the field once again and occasionally chatted to the wind, which gave a bit of variety to the scarecrow's dull life.

The Sly Mouse

A little mouse was sitting in the larder nibbling a piece of cheese. Then the cat crept up to the mouse and tried to catch it.

In mortal fear, the little mouse said, "Well-bred cats wash their mouth and paws before they eat." Taken aback and feeling ashamed, the cat let the mouse go and began to wash itself.

The mouse then siezed its chance and ran as fast as lightning back to its hole. This infuriated the cat who decided that from then on he would always wash after its meal and not before! And if you ever watch a cat you'll see that it's kept it's word!

Whining Walter

Walter was a little boy who whined many times every day. For instance, when he was getting dressed if he could not find his socks he would whine. At breakfast if the milk was too hot, he would whine. If he couldn't find his favourite car in the toy box, he would whine again.

Soon he had earned the nickname "Whining Walter". Of course, this nickname made him whine and whine all the more.

One day a favourite aunt of Walter's had been invited to tea. Walter's mother had laid the table and he helped. He carried plates, spoons and knives to the table and, last of all, he took the lovely cake to the table which his mother had baked especially.

As Walter was carrying it to the table he stumbled, fell over and landed with his face in the cake! His mother hurried over to him and lifted him up. Walter was about to burst into tears at this point when his mother laughed and said, "Just take a look at yourself!" Walter looked in the mirror and saw his face covered in cream, and even he had to laugh.

"You see," said Walter's mother, "it's much better to laugh than to whine and cry! Let's see if we can salvage the cake." Walter's mother then put what she could of the cake back together again and they had a lovely tea with Aunt Joan.

And whenever Walter was about to whine in future his mother would say, "Think of the cake!" and he would stop whining at once and smile.

A Mistake

Mr Wilson has a large, expensive car which he is very proud of. His car is larger, faster and more comfortable than any other car, well, according to Mr Wilson. Yesterday, however, something happened which made him very thoughtful.

Mr Wilson stopped at a garage to fill up with petrol, to check his tyres, water and oil. He paid and then drove off. When he had been travelling along the main road for quite some time he noticed two men in the car behind who kept signalling at him.

"They must want to show me how fast they can go," thought Mr Wilson to himself. And with that he put his foot down on the accelerator. Still the other car remained close behind. This annoyed Mr Wilson, so he drove even faster. But still he could not shake off the car behind. Eventually both cars had to wait at a closed level crossing whilst a train went past.

Mr Wilson got out of his car and went to have a word with the men in the car behind. "Don't bother to try and drive faster than me, because my car is much faster than yours!" said Mr Wilson crossly. The man replied, "We don't want to have a race, all we want to do is give you back your wallet which you left at the petrol station."

Mr Wilson was flabbergasted at this. He thanked the two men very politely and went back to his car, feeling very ashamed of himself.

Helping Out!

"Trust you to get the measles right now when it is so near Easter," said Mummy Easter Bunny to her little boy. "Who will I get to help me give out the Easter Eggs now?" she said to herself, and waggled her long ears as she thought about it. "I'll have to get someone to help me out for a little while," she decided.

Then she remembered that she had helped her cousin the squirrel find his supplies of food during the Winter, perhaps he would help her out now?

She set off at once to the old oak tree where the squirrel family lived. Then she came bounding back full of glee, shouting, "Yippee! the squirrel is coming to help out and he's bringing his wife along to help too!"

So everything went well. Whilst Mummy Easter Bunny painted the eggs, the squirrels took them out and hid them for the children to find on Easter Day!

Small Melanie

Melanie is a very small girl, much smaller than all the other children of her age. That is why she is often teased by the others. "Titchy, tiny Melanie, no-one is as small as you!" called the other children spitefully. They never realised, however, how much their teasing hurt Melanie.

So, one day, she decided to do something about it. She went to the chemist's and asked for something to make her grow taller. The chemist grinned to himself and said, "I'm sorry, young lady, but I have nothing to make you grow taller. Growing comes from nature and I'm sure you'll soon shoot up."

This reply made Melanie very sad, so sad in fact that she forgot to thank the chemist for the barley sugar sweet he gave her. Sadly she went to the playground and watched the other children playing. Suddenly a red ball went whizzing over the fence. The children ran to see where it had landed and realised that it had gone into the garden next door. There was a hole in the fence, so narrow though that only a very small person could fit through it.

"Melanie, do come and help us get the ball!" yelled the children. Melanie squeezed through the hole and retrieved the ball. "What a good job you're so small!" said the children. "Being small can sometimes be better than being tall!" they said. Melanie was overjoyed at this remark and from that day on she was never teased again.

No Time, No Time

"What a beautiful day!" exclaimed the grasshopper joyfully. "I'm going for a walk through the meadow to the stream."

On his way he met a centipede and he said to her, "Come and join me, I'm going to the stream." "No time, no time," was her reply, I must wash one hundred socks and hang them out in the sun to dry."

So the grasshopper continued on his way until he bumped into a snail and called out, "Come and join me, let's go to the stream together!" But the snail replied, "No time, no time, I'm spring cleaning my house today!"

The grasshopper went on his way again and next he bumped into the hedgehog. The grasshopper said, "Come with me to the stream." But the hedgehog replied, "No time, no time. I must sharpen my prickles today, sorry!" And so the grasshopper carried on, then he met a cuckoo. The grasshopper called out to the cuckoo, "Come with me to the stream." And the cuckoo replied, "I'd love to. I've lots of time today." And the two of them went to the stream and had a lovely time just lazing at the water's edge.

Nick's Dream

"Tomorrow, you can help me with the wallpapering," said Nick's mother to her son. "Now, go to sleep and see you in the morning." He soon fell asleep and began to dream of wallpapering.

He took a large pair of scissors and cut and cut, but he did not cut the wallpaper. Instead he cut through the curtains, his trousers and the flowers on the window-sill — everything, absolutely everything was cut up.

Next, he began pasting. He held the brush firmly, and began to paste until the paper was covered. In fact, everything became sticky — the table stuck to the ground, the stool stuck to the wall and the wallpaper stuck to the table!

Then Nick climbed up the step ladder to hang up the wallpaper, but the ladder toppled over and he fell off and landed with a bump on the floor. The boy was totally confused.

Then he heard his mother's voice say, "Nick, time to get up now. We're wallpapering today!" He woke up and hoped that the wallpapering would go better than it had done in his nightmare.

Lisa Falls Asleep

When Lisa went to bed one night she decided to sit and read for a while, as she did not feel at all sleepy. Then the sandman came to her and told her to go to sleep. The sandman visits all children at bedtime.

Lisa began to chat to the sandman and asked him, "Do you visit lots of children as well as me? Do you go and see all the children yourself or do you have helpers? When do you go to sleep? Why do you carry a bag of sand? . . ."

"Stop, stop!" cried the sandman, "I can't answer so many questions at once. Besides I haven't much time. If every child stayed awake as long as you I'd never get round to them all in time. I tell you what, I'll answer just one of your questions every night. Tonight's answer — I've four thousand six hundred and fifty nine children to visit tonight. Do you understand why I'm in such a hurry now?"

Then he sprinkled several grains of sand into Lisa's eyes and she fell asleep straight away.

The Helpful Pedestrian

Once, a man went down to the harbour to watch the fishing boats. Suddenly, a young boy came running up to him, yelling, "My brother, my brother has. . . ." But he was unable to explain fully before the man rushed over to where the boy was pointing. He saw a hat bobbing up and down on the water. "Good heavens, the boy is drowning!" the man called out.

He dived into the sea to save the boy. Although he swam and swam he could not find anyone in the sea. Finally, he swam back to the bank and said to the boy, "I'm sorry, but I can't find your brother anywhere!"

The boy replied, "My brother isn't in the water. He just threw his hat in by accident. That is what I wanted to tell you but you wouldn't let me finish!" Then the boy went on his way, leaving the man soaking wet and totally baffled!

A Long Time Ago

A long, long time ago the job of a night watchman was very important indeed, and different from the job as it is today.

He would go through the streets and would ring his hand bell to let the people know that they should turn out their lamps and blow out the candles. "Why did he do that?" asked Freddie, whose father was explaining about the night watchmen of days gone by.

"He warned the people to turn out their oil lamps and to blow out the candles, because most of the houses were made out of wood in those days and could easily catch fire," explained Freddie's father. He would even sing a song as he went on his rounds. It went something like this . . . "Take care, take care to blow out the candles and turn out the lamps for fire is near!"

So in those days the job of the night watchman was very different but that does not mean that nowadays the job is no longer important. It is just as important, but in a different way.

The Noise In The Bush

One sunny Summer's afternoon when we were sunbathing on the patio, we heard a strange noise coming from the nearby bush. It was a panting sound.

We searched the bush but it was difficult to see anything in the undergrowth. Was it a cat perhaps, or an injured animal?

For a while there was silence and then the panting began again. It was then that my little brother decided to throw water into the bush, to make the mystery animal come out. He did this, and straight away a hedgehog crawled out of the bush, quite unconcerned by the shower of water.

We gave him a saucer of milk which he drank, and then he went on his way to find a dry place to rest!

The New Game

Gordon had invented a wonderful new game. It consisted of standing on the balcony and filling a paper bag with water.

Then he would drop the paper bag onto the street below and watch the water burst out and spray onto the street.

Yesterday however, Gordon had a stroke of bad luck. He filled up the paper bag with water and did not bother to check whether anyone was walking along the pavement below when he threw it over the balcony. "Wamm," the bag burst and water splashed all over an elegantly dressed lady! Her dress was soaked.

Gordon saw all this from the balcony and felt very ashamed and embarrassed.

The Bumble-bee

One sunny Spring day a big, fat bumble-bee flew from flower to flower in the meadow. The more it flew, the noisier its buzzing became. "Why do you make such a loud buzzing noise?" asked the bluebell.

"Why shouldn't I buzz loudly," retorted the bumble-bee, "when all the pollen and nectar has been taken by my relatives!"

"I'll give you some advice," said the bluebell. "You should get up earlier in the morning . . . before your relatives. Remember, the early bird catches the worm!"

"I'll think about that," replied the bumble-bee. "Perhaps it's not such a bad suggestion after all!"

The Recovery

The little girl had been ill for a long time but she was now fully recovered. She went into the garden and said to the swallows, "Swallows, I was very ill, but I'm a lot better now." The swallows were busy collecting food and did not listen to her.

Then the little girl said to the bumble-bee, "Bee, I was very ill, but I'm a lot better now." But the bee was busy collecting pollen and did not listen to the child.

So the child said to the cat, "I was very ill, but I'm a lot better now." But the cat did not listen as it needed to go mousing.

The child turned to the sun and told it that she was better now. The sun stayed with the little girl and shone brightly, to bring back the colour to her pale cheeks.

The Terrier

Scottie is a small terrier dog. He has a long coat and looks very comical and is very playful. His favourite pastime is to sit in the back of the car and watch everything whizzing past.

Yesterday he had a very upsetting experience. As Mr Johnson, Scottie's owner, was driving along he had to brake suddenly — and Scottie was thrown off the back seat and landed between the two front seats!

That was a great shock to his system and from now on he will always sit under Mr Johnson's seat, like a well-behaved dog should!

Catching a Hare

Whenever Richard began to tell a story, his parents would shake their heads in disbelief and say, "That just can't be true! I don't believe you." But still he told the most incredible stories.

One day he told the story of when there was a flood. All the land around was flooded and lots of animals were drowned.

However, there was a hare who was rescued from drowning by sitting on a branch of a tree. Richard said that he noticed the hare shivering from cold and rescued it by rowing up to it in his boat. He lifted the hare off the branch and took it home. He gave it to his little sister as a pet.

"And that's how I caught a hare," said Richard at the end of his story. The hare, however, did not stay for long, and as soon as the flood water had drained away, it returned to the meadow where it was happier.

Baker Street

Diggers and cranes rumbled and clattered on the work site at Baker Street all day long.

In the evening all was quiet once again. The people who lived there looked forward to these peaceful evenings.

But one night the inhabitants were awakened by a loud "Ratta ratta tat!" They all opened their windows and called out to one another, "Who on earth is making that racket at this time of night?" But there was no reply. "It must be a badger making all that noise," said one little boy, "because badgers wake up at night time."

The other neighbours all burst out laughing when they heard this and said, "Why didn't we think of that?" And then they all went back to bed laughing. They never did find out who or what had been making such a noise.

The Spray Telephone

James was having a bath. He splashed about in the water and played with his sailing boat. "Don't forget to wash behind your ears!" his mother called.

Then his father went into the bathroom to play the 'telephone' game. He reluctantly put the hand shower attachment to his ear because he did not really want to play this game. James turned on the water tap so that his father would get sprayed with water. He'll get drenched, James thought. "Turn it off!" yelled his father.

By the time James had turned the tap off, everywhere was wet through. And his father did not know whether to laugh or be cross. James managed to persuade his father to play the 'telephone' game again, as long as he didn't turn the tap on.

The Letter Box

The postman parked his bicycle at the end of the garden path at the forester's house. He was about to post the mail through the letter box when he noticed a sign on it, saying, "Please do not post letters into this box as it is occupied."

"Well, well," thought the postman to himself, "I wonder what is in there?" He looked into the post box and saw five little sparrows waiting for food. "It looks as though the birds are too lazy to build proper nests these days," said the postman to himself.

He knocked on the door of the forester's house whose wife opened the door. She said, "Can you please bring the post to the house from now on as we have a family of birds in the letter box?" The postman agreed to do this as he was very fond of animals and did not want to disturb the birds.

Paul's Find

One day, as he was walking home, Paul found a purse on the pavement containing a lot of money. Just think what he could buy with it? — the ice-skates he had always wanted, a tent, or a toy car or even. . . . Paul was sorely tempted to keep the purse, but he knew that it did not belong to him.

So he handed it in at the nearest shop. As he handed the purse to the shopkeeper, he noticed a shabbily dressed woman at the counter. She came up to Paul and said, "What a good boy you are for bringing back my purse," and then she hugged him because the purse contained all her housekeeping money for the next month. She had four children to bring up.

After school the next day, Paul received a present from the lady whose purse he had found. She had very kindly bought him a football. Paul's mother was very proud of her son for handing in the purse and said to him, "Just imagine, Paul, some children would have just kept the money and spent it secretly!"

Paul realised that doing good created happiness and brought its own rewards.

At the Mill

Once upon a time a wizard disguised as a beggar went walking through the countryside. When he came to a mill he went up to the rich miller and begged him for something to eat. The miller had no time for him and said, "Go away, there are too many of your sort about, I can't feed all of you."

Just at that moment, a poor farmer arrived at the mill with a bag of wheat for grinding. He had heard the harsh words of the miller and he gave the beggar some wheat. In fact, the beggar ate so much wheat that there was not much left for grinding.

The miller could not understand why the farmer had been so kind. Then the farmer put the remainder of the wheat into the mill and began to grind it.

The mill kept on and on grinding, filling so many sacks that the farmer did not know how he would carry it all home, and so he was rewarded by the wizard for his kindness.

Knitting

An old lady was forever knitting. In warm weather she often sat on the bench by the children's playground and knitted.

One day two girls noticed that the old lady was knitting with the same wool, and then after a while she would undo it all and start again. "Why do you do that?" asked the two girls. "I knit for my living, but I haven't enough money to buy new wool all the time," replied the old lady sadly.

So the two girls decided to help her. They collected odd balls of wool that they found lying around their homes and soon they had a great pile to give her. When they gave the wool to the old lady she was overjoyed. She began to knit a patchwork blanket, using all the different pieces of wool.

She wanted to give the blanket to the two girls when she had finished knitting it, but the girls insisted that it should be sold at the school fete. When it was sold the blanket brought in quite a lot of money and the old lady was able to buy enough wool to last for quite some time. She did not have to spend all her time knitting and then unravelling it all to start again.

Leo, the Sad Clown

"I'd like to go as a cowboy like all my friends," whined Leo, as he was getting ready to go to the school's fancy dress party. His mother was putting on his clown make-up and answered, "But Leo, if everyone goes as cowboys it will be boring. You'll look different from everyone else."

Leo didn't really mind being a clown but what did worry him was that all his friends would carry pistols and he would just be wearing a silly suit, and make-up. His mother finished dressing him in his bright costume. With a large white collar and a wig Leo looked wonderful as a clown, and he went off to the party.

Three hours later, when he came home he was beaming all over his face. "Mummy, guess what, I won first prize for the best costume! Look what I won, a cowboy pistol! It was a great party!" he yelled. "I knew you would do well as a clown!" replied his mother. "I bet you're glad you went as a clown and not as a cowboy after all!"

Teddy Goes on Holiday

Andrew was a little boy who loved his teddy bear more than anything else in the world. He took his teddy to bed with him every night and told him all his secrets. Even though the teddy had become rather shabby, Andrew thought he was the best bear in the world!

One Summer, Andrew and his mother went to stay with Aunt Mary who lived up in the mountains, and, of course, the teddy bear went with him. Unfortunately, Andrew forgot to pack him when they went home from the wonderful holiday.

The boy was very upset at forgetting his teddy and he really missed him, especially at night-time. So he wrote to his Aunt Mary asking her to take care of his precious teddy bear until he could go and collect him in a fortnight's time.

When Andrew collected his teddy he thought he was browner than before, probably because he had been on holiday, sunbathing in the hot, mountain sunshine. Andrew was very glad to have his teddy bear back so that he could tell him all his secrets once again.

The Ink Well

A long time ago there used to be an ink well on the top of every school desk, but since cartridge pens and biros were invented there aren't any ink wells on desks anymore.

Sometimes naughty children would dip their pens into the ink and then flick the ink at the teacher when her back was turned and she was writing on the blackboard.

There was one especially naughty girl called Emma who would constantly pelt the teacher with ink, and then get the rest of the class into trouble for it.

So one day, the other pupils decided to put some blotting paper into the ink well. When Emma dipped her pen in, there was no ink left — it had all been absorbed into the blotting paper. This taught her a lesson and from then on she stopped flicking ink at the teacher.

The Baby Hare

One rainy evening, a baby hare sat at the roadside by its mother who had been knocked down by a passing car and was dead. Another car spotted the hare and pulled up.

The driver got out and when he saw the baby hare he carried it back to his car. When the driver arrived home he gave the baby hare to his daschund, Emily who cared for it as if it were her own puppy.

The Ant and the Pigeon

One day, an ant had worked all day long and at the end of the day he longed for a long cool drink, so he went to the bank of a nearby stream.

But he accidentally slipped and fell into the water. The ant would have drowned if a pigeon had not been flying past just at that moment. The pigeon saved the ant's life by throwing a piece of wood which it managed to climb on to and then floated safely back to the bank.

Soon after, the ant saw a hunter about to shoot the pigeon. Just as the hunter was ready to fire, the ant crept into his trousers and made him itch, so he misfired and the pigeon's life was saved.

Rob and the Echo

One day Rob went into the woods and called loudly, "Hello, I'm here!" "I'm here," replied the echo, but Rob did not know or understand about echoes.

"Who are you?" called Rob again. "Who are you?" replied the echo. "You're stupid!" cried Rob angrily. Then he shouted other unpleasant things. But the echo just repeated them all.

Finally, in despair, Rob ran home to his mother and told her about the cheeky voice in the wood. "If you had said nice things to the voice, it would have said them back to you," said his mother smiling. "It was your own echo you were hearing!" she explained.

Dumbo, The Elephant

There was great joy and excitement among the people of a tiny Indian village when Dana, the elephant, gave birth to a baby. The baby elephant was called Dumbo. Dumbo became the children's favourite and every day they would bring him fruit and juicy leaves. When they had fed him, they would ride on his back. Dumbo soon grew into a strong, healthy elephant.

This pleased the men of the village, because they always needed elephants to tear down trees and carry the big tree trunks. However, the men became disappointed because although Dumbo grew up to be strong, his tusks remained too short to carry heavy tree trunks.

But the children didn't mind and said, "Dumbo can be our school bus. He can carry us to school on his back." Everyone agreed to this and Dumbo was happy to take the children to school because they gave him something extra special to eat!

Anna, The Nibbler

All children have a sweet tooth, everyone knows that, but Anna must have the sweetest tooth of all. She is forever nibbling sweets and if she continues she will become as round as a barrel.

She invited all her friends to her birthday party. Her mother baked some special biscuits and cakes and, of course, Anna was at her side all the time! Anna's mother had just popped out of the kitchen for a moment when Anna seized her chance and hastily gobbled down a handful of the delicious biscuit mixture before her mother returned.

Anna's friends came to the party and they gave her some lovely gifts and played games. Then there were the lovely biscuits and cakes to eat but Anna did not enjoy any at all. She had terrible stomach ache! If she had not been so greedy and eaten the mixture, she would have enjoyed the party with the rest of her friends.

Ingrid Finds a Nest

Ingrid was a 'townie' but she had spent quite a long time on her Aunt's farm this Summer and she was beginning to enjoy the country life more with each day that went by. The farmer's wife said to Ingrid one day, "If only I knew where the hens were laying their eggs! Keep your eyes open for their nests, Ingrid!" Ingrid searched with all her cousins for quite a while, but they soon got bored and gave up the hunt for the eggs.

Next morning, Ingrid woke up bright and early, because she could hear the hens clucking outside her window. There, in the field, were lots of hens. Ingrid rushed out in her jeans and wellingtons to see if she could find the eggs. And soon she found a nest containing at least twenty eggs. Ingrid took them to her Aunt who thanked her heartily for finding the eggs. Now they could all have eggs for breakfast.

Later she gave Ingrid a new doll for finding the eggs. "This doll is to remind you of your stay with us," said her Aunt, who wished that Ingrid did not have to go back to the town.

Ingrid Makes Butter

One day, Ingrid was allowed to climb high up the mountains with Peter, the farmer's son. The climb was steep, but well worth the effort just for the wonderful view from the top.

After walking for three hours, the two children reached the hut at the top of the mountain where Peter's Grandma lives. She spends the whole of the summer in the hut looking after the cows that graze on the lush mountain pasture. She milks the cows and makes butter and cheese.

"How do you make butter?" asked Ingrid curiously. Peter's grandmother showed her the butter churn on the kitchen table. "You have to turn the handle of the churn for at least one hour to make the cream into butter," explained Peter's Grandma.

She let Ingrid have a go. Ingrid turned the handle round and round until her hand hurt. "You're turning it too fast, do it gently and smoothly then you won't get tired so quickly," said Peter's grandmother. Ingrid did this and sure enough, after a while she had made butter for the very first time.

Ingrid was very proud of the butter and thought how amazed her friends in the town would be if they knew that she had made it. They all thought that butter came from shops!

Ears of Corn

A long, long time ago, the ears of corn grew far more corn than they do now. They used to grow up the whole of the stalk. The people had more than enough corn and so did not take much notice of it.

One day, when a mother and daughter were walking through a corn field, the girl fell in a puddle and dirtied her hand. Her mother simply tore a handful of corn out of the field and wiped her daughter's hands clean.

A wizard who was in charge of the corn fields saw this and was furious. He said, "From now on, no more ears of corn are to grow on the stalks, since no-one appreciates it." The people who heard the wizard say this were frightened and went down on their knees and begged, "Please let there be some corn on the stalks, so that we can at least feed the hens with it, for they are not the guilty ones."

So the wizard took pity on the hens and let there be a little bit of corn on the stalks. And that is how it is today.

Catching a Crocodile

"Tell me Ben, do you know how to catch a crocodile?" asked Bill. "You take a net and throw it over his head and haul him in," answered Ben. "No, you're wrong," replied Bill.

"What you do is take a very boring book, a pair of binoculars, a pair of tweezers and a match box and then you go to the River Nile in Egypt, because that is where the crocodiles live. You sit down on the bank of the Nile and read the book which is so boring that it makes you fall asleep.

When you are fast asleep, the crocodile comes and reads the boring book until, he, too falls asleep. Because you fell asleep first you wake up before the crocodile. Then you look through the binoculars the wrong way round so that the crocodile looks very small, so small, that you can take the tweezers, pick up the sleeping crocodile and put it in the match box. Then you have caught the crocodile," said Bill.

"Great story!" laughed Ben, "but I know a better way — put the crocodile in the bath and pull the plug out and then you have caught the crocodile!" "Oh no!" exclaimed Bill, "that's enough of these corny stories!"

The Wren as King

A long, long time ago the birds decided to choose a King. One sunny, May morning they all met, the eagle, the blue tit, the lark, the cuckoo and all the other birds.

They decided that the bird who could fly the highest would be King. They all took off at once, and there was a tremendous fluttering of feathers as they flew into the sky. The eagle soared the highest, so high in fact, that he could almost reach the clouds. All the small birds sank to the ground because their little wings could not carry them very high. In the end all the small birds shouted, "Eagle, you are our King!"

But one little bird, the wren, chirped, "Oh, but I'd really like to be King, just because I can't fly so high doesn't mean to say I wouldn't make a good King. Please let me be King."

The other birds thought about this for a long time and finally decided that they could have two Kings, one for the larger birds and one for the smaller birds. And so the wren's wish came true and it became King.

The Trouble-Maker

Aunt Jane was our favourite aunt and we loved visiting her. Her house always smelt of lavender, apples and homemade cakes. But another attraction for us was her brightly coloured jug.

Aunt Jane always had a lot of patience. She did not mind our tricks, but on one occasion our younger brother, Roger, went too far.

Aunt Jane did not mind us hiding her shoes, or sewing up the arm hole of a shirt, but when Roger poured ink into her favourite jug and then put her gold watch into the ink, she was very cross indeed.

She called Roger a trouble-maker and made him clean up the mess. He had to scrub and scrub until he had removed all the ink from the jug. As for the watch, well, he had to take it to the jewellers to be mended because the ink had seeped in and stopped it from working.

Selling 'Betsie'

Mr Robson had an old blue car called Betsie, that had always been very reliable. He had taken very good care of her. Then, one day he said to his wife, "Joan, that car is getting old, I think it's time we sold her and bought a new one."

Betsie overheard this conversation and it made her very sad. Mr Robson put an advertisement in the paper which read, "Well maintained blue car for sale."

It was not long before a gentleman came along to look at Betsie. He inspected her carefully, whilst Mr Robson explained all her good points.

Then suddenly there was a funny noise, "psssch . . ." it went, and the air came out of Betsie's tyres. They went completely flat, leaving Mr Robson to say, "I can't understand why that's happened, it's never happened before." The gentleman went away. He didn't want to buy a car that suddenly lets its tyres down, did he?

Betsie Battles On

The next day Mr Robson put another advertisement in the paper — "Well maintained blue car for sale." Again it did not take long for someone to come round to look at Betsie.

Again Mr Robson emphasised all Betsie's good points whilst the client inspected her. Mr Robson had pumped up the four tyres. Then, suddenly, a mudguard dropped off and fell on the client's foot! "Ouch," he yelled and jumped back a few steps.

"I can't understand why that's happened, it's never happened before," said Mr Robson in disbelief. The client, however, left at that moment, he didn't want to buy a car that suddenly loses a mudguard!

Betsie Doesn't Give Up

The next day Mr Robson put the advertisement in the paper again — "Well maintained blue car for sale." And again Mr Robson did not have long to wait for a customer. This time a lady came to look at Betsie.

Mr Robson had fixed the mudguard back onto the car and again he mentioned all the car's good points. The lady walked around the car, checking its paintwork and tyres. She looked very pleased and then the windscreen wipers suddenly sprayed her with water. She was soaked from head to toe.

"I can't understand why that has happened, it has certainly never happened before!" exclaimed Mr Robson, scratching his head. The lady who had wanted to buy Betsie went away. She did not want to buy a car that suddenly spurted out water!

Betsie Tries Again

The next day, Mr Robson put the advertisement in the paper again — "Well maintained blue car for sale." It was not long before someone came to look at her. This time the client asked about her petrol consumption and was delighted with the answers.

Then, in the middle of the conversation, Betsie started her horn — To-toot-toot, she went. "I can't understand why that's happened, it's never happened before!" exclaimed Mr Robson. The man left at once. He did not want to buy a car that suddenly starts the horn by itself.

Betsie's Last Attempt

The next day, the advertisement was put in the paper again — "Well-maintained blue car for sale." Again, it did not take long for someone to come along to look at the car.

This time a fat, old lady came to have a look. She decided to go on a test drive in Betsie before she finally made her mind up whether to buy her or not. Mr Robson agreed to this and got in the passenger seat beside her.

They set off, but all Betsie would do was to drive round and round in a circle and the fat, old lady was thrown from side to side! "I can't understand why this has happened, it's never happened before!" said Mr Robson completely baffled. The fat, old lady left at once. She did not want to buy a car that does nothing but go round and round in circles!

The Sausage

"Hey, Sam, take a look at what Grandma's sent me — a massive sausage!" shouted Ben to his friend.

"Crikey, Ben, it's almost two metres long! Can I smell it?" asked Sam.

The two of them sniffed the sausage to see if it was a salami sausage.

"I'm not sure what it is," said Ben. "We'd better taste it to make sure."

So both of them began to taste the sausage. It tasted so good, that they had eaten more than half of it. "Stop!" yelled Sam. "We'll soon have eaten it all!"

But Ben did not listen to his friend and he carried on eating it. Soon it was all eaten up and they never did find out whether it was a salami or not!

Betsie Wins!

Mr Robson is at his wits end by now. He does not bother to put the advertisement in the paper again because he can see that Betsie does not want to be sold.

"Joan, it's no use, we'll just have to keep Betsie. After all, where would we find such a loyal, reliable car as our Betsie?" Mr Robson said to his wife.

Betsie was overjoyed when she heard this. She then promised to drive Mr and Mrs Robson safely during the years ahead.

The Calculator

Martin was busy doing his maths homework. He hated doing mathematics because he had to think so hard and it took so long!

Suddenly an idea came to him. He crept into his father's study and took the calculator out of his desk. He knew how to use it because his father had shown him. Now he would be able to do his homework in no time! 345+50, 267+80, the calculator worked out these sums instantly.

When he had finished his homework, he returned the calculator to his father's desk. He then took his homework to show to his mother. She checked everything and said, "Very good. Excellent!" For a while Martin carried on in this way, using the calculator secretly.

Then one day Martin came home from school in tears. He had got an 'E' in the Maths test! His mother was very puzzled and upset when she heard the news because she thought he had been doing really well. So Martin had to own up that he had used the calculator to do his homework. His mother said, "Oh Martin! You are a silly boy, you should only use the calculator after you've learnt to do sums by yourself!"

So Martin had to work all the sums out on his own from then on and when he got a bit stuck his mother would help him, and he gradually got better at mathematics.

The Sledge

There were fun and games on the hill that was used for sledging. Lots of children were having great fun sledging and snowballing. There were even some skiiers on the slope and they had made a ski jump.

Then four boisterous boys arrived with a very long wooden sledge. They decided to go over the ski jump on the sledge. Going as fast as they could, they leapt over the jump and then landed in the snow! The sledge had overturned leaving the four boys tipped over in the snow!

The other children roared with laughter as the four boys tried to climb back on their sledge. They didn't try that jump again but had fun on the slopes.

Alex and Santa Claus

Alex came out of school feeling very fed up. He had got yet another bad mark in the mathematics test and he could not do the homework that the teacher had set.

As he did not feel like going home straight away, he decided to go for a walk through the town which had been decorated for Christmas. He stopped at the department store when he saw Santa Claus.

Alex went into the store to take a closer look at Santa. He saw him handing out sweets to all the children and wishing them a Merry Christmas. Santa noticed Alex looking very miserable and he went up to him and asked him what the matter was. The boy explained that he was having great difficulty with maths and Santa very kindly explained to Alex how to tackle his homework.

As Santa Claus explained the basic principles to Alex, it all became much clearer to him. Santa told him not to give up trying at mathematics. "You must keep plodding away, it will be worth while in the end," said Santa. Alex thanked Santa Claus for his help and went home feeling greatly relieved. "Where on earth have you been?" asked Alex's mother. She had been very worried about her son, and had been on the point of going into the town to see if she could find him there.

"Santa Claus has been giving me an extra maths lesson," said Alex. His mother just looked at him and Alex could see that she just did not believe him. She ordered him to bed at once because she thought he must be getting flu!

Collecting Twigs

"It will soon be Christmas," said Mrs Jackson to her children. "Let's go and collect some twigs today. It would be nice to put some twigs in a vase and also have some to light the fire," added Mrs Jackson. "Oh yes let's do that," replied Lucy excitedly. She loved going for long walks in the woods with her mother and little brother, Tom.

They set off for the woods and soon they had found lots of twigs and some branches of holly to take home. They had dressed up warmly because it was icy cold outside.

Tom decided to throw snowballs at Lucy when they had collected enough twigs. He threw a huge one at her which hit her arm. "Ouch!" yelled Lucy, "that hurt." Then she picked up a handful of twigs and ran after her brother, waving the twigs at him. She chased him all the way home but did not catch him. The chase had certainly warmed them up on this cold, wintry day.

The Dust Dwarf

Once when a lady was sweeping her kitchen floor, she heard a little voice cry out, "Leave me alone, don't sweep me up, I've done you no harm." "Who are you then?" asked the lady, astonished. "I'm the dust dwarf, I love dusty corners, especially those that are never cleaned!" replied the dust dwarf.

"Well, I'm afraid I'm Spring cleaning the whole house," said the lady. "I can't abide specks of dust, you'll have to go!" "Oh but you will be making a big mistake, if you sweep me up. If you give me a little corner to live in I'll bring you good luck," begged the dust dwarf.

He pleaded and pleaded with the lady to let him stay and in the end she gave in, and said he could stay in the corner behind the dresser. The dust dwarf promised to stay there and never to wander out into the kitchen.

From then on, the lady and her family prospered. From time to time, she thought to herself, "If the other women in the neighbourhood knew of this speck of dust, what would they think? But who knows, perhaps they have one in their homes and do not know it!"

Lazy Marianne

Although Marianne is a good natured girl, she is very lazy. She is forever putting things off and saying, "Oh, I'll do that later!" One day at the beginning of December, Marianne's mother suggested that she should crochet her Grandmother a kettle holder for Christmas. "Yes, I'll do that, but not now. I'll do it later," replied Marianne.

On the 6th of December, it was Marianne's birthday and she received lots of presents including a huge ball of wool on which was placed a card saying, "Marianne, start crocheting now, then the kettle holder will be ready in time for Christmas."

She began at once. Every day Marianne would find a little present in her work basket — a bar of chocolate, some marzipan or toffees. These presents encouraged her to work even harder. She finished the kettle holder just in time for Christmas and no-one could call her a lazy bones any more. Her Grandmother was delighted with her present, because homemade presents are always the best.

Test of Courage

"Bet you can't sleep out in the garden all night long by yourself," said Jane to her sister Rosie. "I'll bet you three stamps that you can't stay out there all night long," said her brother, as they were both keen stamp collectors.

That evening, Rosie put her camp bed in the garden and when it became dark, she got into her sleeping bag and snuggled down for a good night's sleep. At first she thought it marvellous to breathe in the fresh air.

A little later she thought she saw dark shapes moving in the shadows. The darkness made everything strange and frightening. In the end, Rosie could not stay outside any longer and crept back into the house to sleep in her own bed. Her brother and sister saw her go back to her bedroom and, of course, Rosie lost the bet and didn't get the three extra stamps for her stamp collection.

The Sandman

The Sandman creeps up to little children every night to check that they are fast asleep. If a child is not asleep when he looks in, he will throw a few grains of the finest sand into his or her eyes to make the child sleepy.

One evening, however, the Sandman was late because he had messed around and taken a long time in filling his sack with sand. As he had then hurried to make up lost time, he caught his sack on a rosebush and the thorns tore a hole in his sack, and the sand began to leak out.

So when he saw the children who had not fallen asleep, he was unable to make them sleep because his sack was empty, all the sand had gone!

However, he had a good idea — he would sing the children to sleep. He began to sing the lullaby "Rock-a-bye baby in the tree top . . ." and then he would quietly tiptoe away to the next child on his round when he was sure that the child was sleeping soundly.

The next night, the Sandman did not have to sing because his sack had been mended. The Sandman was very glad because he was beginning to get a sore throat from all this singing! He wasn't very good at singing anyway, so he felt happier with his sack full of sand again.

Where are the Glasses?

"Where have I put my glasses?" asked Grandma, as she searched for them under all the cushions. She searched all over, looked for them in the most unlikely places but could not find them anywhere.

In the end, she searched through the pockets of her apron, but no luck. Then her granddaughter came up to her and said, "Don't you know, Grandma your glasses are on the end of your nose. You're wearing them!" "Well whatever next!" said Grandma, "I really must be getting old if I think I'm not wearing my glasses when I've got them on the end of my nose!"

Talking Whilst Eating

"Don't speak with your mouth full, Richard," said his father for the third time. "Firstly, no-one can tell what you are saying and secondly you could end up with food stuck in your windpipe, which is very dangerous as it will make you choke."

Richard did not listen to what his father said. Instead he carried on eating and talking at the same time. Then he began to cough and splutter, and he went redder and redder. His mother had to pat him on the back which helped him.

He stopped coughing and spluttering and got his breath back. "I did warn you about choking but you insisted on talking with your mouth full!" said Richard's father. "I know, I'm sorry I didn't listen to you," replied Richard feeling very ashamed of himself.

The Broom

There was once a lady who kept her broom in a corner of the kitchen. The broom stayed in that corner for what seemed like a life-time. It became very bored and began to moan, "Will I be in this corner forever? I want to get out and see the world!"

Then the lady took the broom out of its corner. "Great!" thought the broom to itself, "I'll definitely get to see the world now!" But, instead, the broom was set to work sweeping the floor, under the table, behind the benches, in all the corners of the kitchen and even over the outside steps.

That evening, the broom was very tired and was glad to be able to rest in the corner once more. From then on, the broom very rarely had thoughts of seeing the world.

At The Garden Gate

Timothy was a little boy who lived in a cottage in a village. In front of the cottage was a lovely garden. Timothy loved to spend his days just looking out over the garden gate.

He loved to chat to all the people as they went past. He would chat to the postman. The dustbin men were also his good friends and so was the next door neighbour, who would always wink at Timothy as he took his dog for a walk.

Then one day, Timothy was leaning over the fence when he noticed a removal van parked next door. Some new neighbours were moving in. Timothy shouted, "Hello there!" and a little boy, about the same age as Timothy, shouted back, "Well, hello! My name is John!"

Soon the two boys became great friends. And they would often spend their time leaning over the garden gate, watching the world go by and chatting to the other neighbours.

King of the Kitchen

At midnight, the kitchen came to life. All the kitchen equipment decided to choose a King of the kitchen. Immediately, confusion broke out as everyone started to shout at once. "I can fry the breakfasts," said the frying pan, "so I should be King!"

"I'm much more important than you," said the kettle, "after all I boil the water for the tea! Besides I can whistle too."

"I boil potatoes and vegetables," said the saucepan, "so I should be King especially as I've so much more experience in the kitchen."

"Stop quarrelling you lot," broke in the cooker. "I'm the King of the kitchen and always will be. For who heard of a kitchen without a cooker, it's like a house without windows!" The others agreed with the cooker and stopped their quarrelling — the cooker was indeed the King!

Starting School

It was Dave's first day at school. He carried his new satchel on his back and he held his mother's hand as he went into the school playground. He was very excited about all the new things he would see and do there.

A friendly teacher greeted him and he met lots of other children. The teacher told lovely stories and Dave thoroughly enjoyed the whole day.

When he got home, he talked of nothing but school, until he went to bed completely exhausted.

The next day, his mother woke him and said, "Dave, it's time to get up. You've got to go to school again today!"

Dave had not realised that he had to go to school every day. One day of school had been more than enough!

The Sweet Eater

Pamela was a little girl who was always nibbling. She was forever rummaging through the kitchen cupboards for food.

One day she discovered a jar of raspberry jam in the larder. Mmmm . . . what a lovely smell. Pamela just could not resist it. She dipped her finger into the jam, not once but several times, and then she wiped her mouth on her apron and crept out of the kitchen but first she put the jar of jam back in the larder. Her mother would never know that she had been at the jam.

At tea-time, Pamela's mother asked, "Well, Pamela did you like the raspberry jam?" Pamela went bright red and wondered how on earth her mother knew that she had eaten the jam. "Just take a look at yourself in the mirror!" said her mother. And when Pamela looked in the mirror, she saw that she had raspberry stains all around her mouth!

The New Bicycle

The children's toys stood next to the car in the garage. The tractor had a mudguard missing. Next to the tractor stood a rusty old tricycle and a scooter.

Then one day another toy arrived, this time, a shiny, brand new bicycle. "Who are you then?" asked the tricycle curiously. "Can't you see," said the tractor, "it is such a superior bike that it won't lower itself to talk to us." "We're obviously too shabby," continued the tricycle, "but just you wait until it looks like us!"

The bicycle remained silent and proud. How long would it stay so clean and new?

Mark at the Circus

Have you ever been to the circus? Yes? Then you already know what it is like in a circus tent. There is the ring in the middle of the tent where the artists perform and then there are wooden benches set out for all the spectators to sit. The benches are put round so that everyone can see the ring.

Mark went to the circus with his aunt. He clapped his hands and jumped out of his seat whenever he liked an act. His eyes shone with happiness. He especially enjoyed the chimpanzees and leapt out of his seat to applaud and. . . .

"Mark where are you?" called his aunt. Mark's seat was empty. "Here I am!" yelled Mark. What had happened? Mark had jumped up and down in excitement and had then fallen down the gap between the seats. He quickly climbed back into his seat.

"Have you hurt yourself?" asked Mark's aunt. "No, the ground is soft, but you wouldn't believe what is down here. There's sweet papers, coke cans, programmes and cigarette ends!" said Mark. "And sometimes even little boys!" added his aunt laughing.

The Good-natured Dragon

There was once a King who was very worried because a fire-breathing dragon lived in the forests of his kingdom. None of the King's subjects had the courage to catch the dragon, so the King had to look elsewhere for someone brave enough to hunt the dragon.

One day, a Prince from a neighbouring country arrived at the palace and said to the King, "Your Majesty, I will catch the monster for you. I'm not afraid of it."

The Prince searched through the forests until he saw the dragon sitting at the edge of a brook. When he looked closer he saw that the dragon was crying. "Why are you crying?" asked the Prince. "Why shouldn't I cry, when no-one dares come near me and no-one loves me. I look awful, but I wouldn't harm anyone. I only eat grass and leaves, and I only breathe out fire occasionally."

So the Prince tied a cord around the dragon's neck and led it back to the palace. The people were astonished as they saw the Prince leading the dragon through the streets!

The Prince presented the good-natured dragon to the King and said, "Your Majesty, this is the dragon. This beast would not harm a fly and he has told me that his greatest wish is to serve you at the palace."

When the King had recovered from the shock of seeing the dragon, he said, "It can remain here with me and make itself useful. All the other Kings will be very envious of my new pet!"

And so the dragon stayed and lit all the ovens in the palace with his jet of fire.

Bird Talk

"Why do swallows gather on the wires every day in the Autumn?" asked the blue-tit. "We practise flying with our fledglings," said the swallow, "before we fly off to the south." "Why do you fly south every year when it is nice here?" asked the blue-tit.

"We can't find any food here in the Winter," replied the swallow. "But that's not true," said the blue-tit. "I find enough food from the fir cones, and the bird tables in the gardens. Stay here for a while and I'll show you my favourite eating place, there is bound to be something you like."

The swallow then asked, "Are there live flies and midges on these food tables?" "Of course not, but there's plenty of grain," replied the blue-tit. "But I don't like grain," said the swallow shaking his head. "You are fussy then, aren't you!" exclaimed the blue-tit.

"No, not really. It's just that swallows are meat eaters," answered the swallow. "That's a shame," retorted the blue-tit. "It means that you have to fly away for the Winter because you don't get flies and midges here." "And another thing," said the swallow as he flew off, "we only eat flies that we catch whilst we're flying!"

Helping the Snails

Ann noticed that the farm's tractor knocked down and killed lots of snails as it went along the path between two fields. Whenever the snails wanted to cross from one field to another they were in a lot of danger when crossing over the path.

So Ann shouted to the snails, "Hey, you snails, this path is too dangerous to cross! Stay on the other side!" But the snails did not understand this. The next day many of them lay dead on the path.

Then Ann decided to put up a sign which said, "Look out! Don't go on the path! Danger!" But that did not help either since the snails could not read.

Finally, Ann painted a picture of giant tractor tyres and lots of squashed snails. She then put it at the side of the path. Since then only a few snails have been run over.

Ann is convinced that the snails must have understood the picture, or could it be that the tractor driver has taken more care since seeing the picture.

The Sleeping Giant

A giant was sleeping one day. He snored so loudly that he made all the trees shake for miles around. A farmer went along the path near the sleeping giant.

When he got close to the giant, he mistook him for a mountain and went over him with his horse and cart. When he reached the giant's nose, he said, "Which one of these two tunnels should I take?"

He decided on the right one and steered his horse into it. The wheels of the cart tickled the giant so much that he let out an almighty sneeze — which blew the farmer and his horse out of the tunnel and into the air. "I'm never going through a tunnel again!" exclaimed the farmer, and steered his horse and cart back down to the path.

At The Cinema

Matthew works hard and is a friendly chap but people say that he hasn't got all his "marbles". What they mean by that is that he's not very bright.

One day, Matthew went to the cinema for the first time. He sat down in his seat and then because it was so warm he took off his coat.

When he sat down again he fell on the floor. Feeling very cross, he stood up and punched the person sitting behind him. "That's for putting my seat up when I stood up!" said Matthew. How was he to know that the seats in a cinema go up on their own?

The Piggy Bank

John was given a piggy bank from his Grandma for his fifth birthday. He decided to save all his five pence pieces in it.

From time to time, he would count up his money to see how much he had saved.

Then his mother urgently needed some change for the telephone and she said to the boy, "John, could you change this fifty pence piece for ten five pences?" John watched in astonishment as his mother took away his five pences and gave him just one fifty pence piece in return. "Now I've got less money than I had before!" whined John. He couldn't understand that he was just as rich as before. He still had the same amount of money — because one fifty pence piece is the same value as ten five pences!

The Advent Calendar

"Mummy, how many days are there until Christmas?" This is the question that mothers are asked again and again throughout advent. When Christmas was approaching one year, a mother thought to herself, "Oh no, they will start pestering me again, asking when Christmas is coming. I'll have to think up an idea to stop all the questions."

So she sat down, took a piece of card and drew twenty four little boxes, one for each day in December until Christmas Day. She gave every box a number, and then decided to put a little surprise in each of them — a chocolate or a jelly baby or a mint.

Now the children would be satisfied with a sweet every day and would not need to ask when it was Christmas. Since then, the mother made a new advent calendar every year and soon all the other mothers throughout the world copied her.

There are calendars which look like houses with twenty four windows to open. An especially nice advent calendar is one in the shape of a Christmas tree. Some advent calendars have a rhyme or a colourful picture behind the doors. Every calendar is slightly different, but they all have the same aim — to make the days before Christmas pass quickly.

Keeping Quiet

Paul's father has bought a holiday chalet in Austria. He wanted to take a television set to the chalet when they went there for the Summer. He packed it in a large, strong box and the whole family set off for Austria.

On the journey, he said to his children, "Now none of you say anything about the television at the border! I don't want to have to declare it because I will have to pay duty on it." The children agreed to keep quiet about the television and soon they arrived at the customs border.

"Have you anything to declare?" asked the Customs Officer and bent down to look into the car. "We mustn't say anything about the television," said Paul innocently, as the Customs Officer looked at the forms. He had given the game away! Paul's father had to open the box, and declare the television.

Of course, his father was furious when he got back into the car. But Paul did not think it fair that he should be punished for telling the truth. After all, you are not supposed to tell lies, but his father had done — was that right? What do you think?

Going to the Opera

"Well Robert, we're off now," said his parents who just popped into his bedroom to say goodnight.

"Don't read for too long and turn out your light before you go to sleep."

"Where are you going?" asked Robert. "You're both looking very smart."

"We're going to the opera," said Robert's father.

"What's the opera?" asked Robert.

"Well the opera is a play in which the actors not only speak but sing, and the orchestra plays," replied his mother.

"Do they sing pop songs?" asked Robert.

"No, an opera is made up of serious music. In fact, it's about time we took you with us. But not tonight so go to sleep and sweet dreams. We'll tell you all about it in the morning."

"Night night," said Robert yawning, for the conversation had made him sleepy.

Sweet Dreams

The nights just before Christmas are very hectic for the Sandman. The children cannot sleep because they are so excited at the thought of Father Christmas and all the presents!

So the Sandman uses his best and finest sand to send them to sleep. But it soon gets used up. The Sandman has no more sand left, what can he do now? He decides to enlist the help of his friend the Dreamman.

He says to the Dreamman, "I know that you work much later than I do, but could you make an exception just this once? I'd like you to come on my rounds with me to help put the children to sleep because I've no sand left and cannot get the children to go to sleep."

The Dreamman agrees and the Sandman goes on his rounds with the Dreamman who hides the sweetest of dreams under the children's pillows — Dreams of Christmas.

My name is Helen and I am nine years old. A few weeks ago our teacher brought a new pupil into our class and said, "This is Nana, she is from Greece. She has only just arrived in England and she cannot speak much English at all, so speak slowly and clearly to her."

I liked Nana at once. She had lovely long, black hair and large dark eyes. The next day I asked her, "What are you doing after school tomorrow when you've finished your homework?" "I look after brother," came the reply.

"We could both look after him," I suggested. She agreed to this and the next day we both looked after her little brother called Demis. He cried when he first saw me but Nana comforted him with words I had never heard before.

Then we went to the playground and met up with Jane, Christine and Liz from our class at school. "Look at Helen mixing with the new girl!" they said jeering. Then they came closer and made lots of hurtful remarks.

Then Demis started to cry again. "Come home," said Nana. On the way home she was very quiet and I did not know what to say to her. It had not been a very successful afternoon! I suggested she came round to my house with her little brother, after school the next afternoon.

The next day when I looked for Nana during the lunch break, I found her with Jane, Christine and Liz. They were whispering together and talking quietly with Nana, who just looked helplessly at me. When the others saw me they became silent. I asked Nana, "What do they want with you?"

"No understand," she replied.

The next afternoon Nana did not come to my house which made me very sad. The day after that she was with the other girls in the playground and refused to talk to me.

After school, Nana ran home so fast that I could hardly catch her. "What's the matter, Nana, why are you running away?" I asked.

"I — home — no time," was the reply.

"But aren't you coming to my house today?" I asked.

"No, no, work, work," replied Nana.

"What's the matter with her," I wondered. And I decided to go to her house the next day.

When I knocked on Nana's door I felt very nervous. Her mother answered the door. I recognised her at once since she had the same kind of long, black hair and dark eyes as Nana.

"I'm Helen, I'm in Nana's class at school," I said. Then I noticed that there were tears in Nana's mother's eyes. "Why do that, Nana?" she asked and I saw Nana standing behind her mother, with short hair! She'd cut off her long hair! It looked dreadful because she had obviously done it herself, but why?

"Me short hair like Christine and Liz," said Nana proudly. "But your long hair was so lovely," I said and her mother nodded in agreement. Then her mother explained to me that the other girls had suggested that Nana cut off her hair because in England short hair is much more fashionable. They had said that Nana looked as though she came from a poor village in Greece.

"We not poor, my father work hard, we not from village, we from city," said Nana. I was furious with Christine and Liz for making Nana cut her lovely, long hair.

I was determined to settle this matter once and for all, so that the three school girls, Liz, Christine and Jane wouldn't feel smug about Nana's dreadful appearance.

I asked Nana's mother if she could come to my house for a couple of hours. She agreed and I took Nana home to my mother who was a hairdresser.

She tidied up Nana's hair and made it look more fashionable. Soon Nana looked much prettier. "Nana, your school friends were only jealous of your lovely long hair, that's why they told you to have it cut," said my mother.

Then I took Nana home and her mother thanked me for helping her. She also told me to thank my mother for cutting Nana's hair so well.

The next day when we both went into the classroom it was marvellous to see the puzzled faces of Christine, Liz and Jane when they saw Nana's smart, new hairstyle.

Nana had won! From then on, she was accepted by the rest of the class. She soon had lots of friends, but I became her best friend and we had lots of happy times together.

The Witch's Chair

Max the dwarf had stayed with the friendly witch Rosa for several months now and had learnt lots of spells. One day Rosa said, "Tomorrow, I'm going to the witches' meeting on the mountain. You'll have to stay here on your own for a few days and take care of the house."

Then she fetched her witch's broom but it broke in two. "Rats and gobbledeygook!" exclaimed Rosa. "Why did that have to happen just when I want to fly off to the meeting?"

"Couldn't you mend it?" suggested Max. "You can never replace a witch's broom — once broken that's it!" said Rosa sharply. She stood there deep in thought for several

minutes and called out, "I've got it! I can use the chair. I can turn it into a flying chair and go on that. It will be much more comfortable than an old broom. I'll put the suggestion forward at the meeting that we include a spell for mending brooms in the Big Book of Spells."

Then she uttered the magic words, "Abra cadabra . . . hey presto chair fly!" At once the chair turned into a magic flying chair and away she went to the meeting. She looked rather odd flying away on an old chair, but just as spectacular as the other witches on their brooms. The chair was much more comfortable than a broom! Rosa was very pleased with her new invention.

The Red Balloon

Next to the roundabout on the fairground was a bunch of brightly coloured balloons. In the middle of the bunch was a bright red one that boasted, "I'm more beautiful than the rest of you. I'm the fattest, roundest and reddest of all."

The others were fed up with hearing this and said, "What is so special about you then? You are still a balloon like the rest of us!"

At that, the red balloon was offended and refused to speak to the others anymore. A wasp came and sat on the red balloon. It stung him, and . . . pafff! The red balloon had burst! It fell to the earth slowly and was no longer a big, round balloon but a small burst balloon!

"The wasp obviously thought that it was the best balloon!" said the other balloons, delighted at the red balloon's downfall!

Weather Talk

"Do you know how you get rain?" asked Bill. His friend Ben shook his head and said, "No, I've no idea how you get rain."

"Well, listen then. Some mountains are so high that they can tickle the clouds with their peaks. The clouds are very ticklish and they start to shake with laughter, and they shake out all the water — onto you and me."

Ben answered, "Is that true, what you said about the rain?"

"No, what I said about the rain and the mountains is not true, but it sounds good doesn't it?" said Bill smiling to himself.

Ben felt very confused because now he really wanted to know how rain was made. Bill could not explain how rain was really made. So Ben decided to ask his teacher the next day. Do you know how rain is made?

Rachel Cooks Tea

Mother was ill in bed with flu. Rachel her daughter, decided to take over.

She went into the kitchen, put on the apron and said, "Tonight I'm making the tea!" Her father and little brother, Robert, were very impressed. "What are you making for tea then?" they asked. "Scrambled eggs," came the reply.

She beat three eggs and a little milk together, added a pinch of salt and heated the fat in the pan and stirred in the egg mixture. Soon the scrambled eggs were ready. Robert tasted his first and exclaimed, "Ugh! it tastes horrible!" Her father added, "Our little chef has mixed the salt with sugar!"

Rachel went back into the kitchen to see if she really had put sugar in the egg mixture. She spotted her mistake — she had not looked at the label on the jar. "It's not so easy to replace Mummy after all," she thought to herself.

The Doorbell Game

Carl had thought up a new game — ringing on people's doorbells. Of course it was not a new game. Lots of mischievious little boys have been playing this sort of trick for a long time.

Carl would ring the bell and then he would run and hide, and watch the person answer the door.

He had to wait ages at one door before anybody answered it. Then an old lady opened the door and said, "You're a kind boy, I thought it was somebody playing a trick on me. You know there are some naughty boys who think it's fun to ring people's door bells and then run off and hide before the person answers. I find it so difficult getting about that I need to use a stick."

Then she gave Carl a bar of chocolate. Carl went redder and redder in the face at this because he felt so ashamed of himself. He had been playing tricks on her too, just like the other boys. But Carl was very quick witted and thought up a good idea to get him out of this awkward situation. He suggested that he did a few errands for the old lady.

From then on he went shopping for the old lady every week and they became great friends. Carl stopped ringing on people's doorbells. He had learnt his lesson!

The Three Brothers

Once there were three brothers who put their boots out at Christmas Eve for Father Christmas to fill with presents. The eldest brother put his father's huge boots out, the second brother his own dirty boots, and the youngest one put out his newly cleaned boots.

The next day, Christmas Day, the eldest brother found a few sweets and a note in his boots saying, "I never leave much in such big boots."

The middle brother found some biscuits and a chocolate in his dirty boots, along with a note which read, "Clean your boots then you'll be given more."

The youngest brother was amazed to find his boots filled with all kinds of toys and goodies. His note read, "He who cleans his own boots and then puts them out is never forgotten by Father Christmas." I think I know what the other brothers will do next year!

The Stubborn Marmot

"I don't want to go to sleep for the Winter," said the young marmot. "I want to stay up and play. Such a long sleep will be so boring!"

"But the Winter sleep is necessary," said his mother, "everything will be covered in snow and we won't be able to find any food."

But the young marmot was very stubborn and would not listen to his mother's advice. Whilst the others all began to prepare for the sleep, making the nest soft and comfortable, the young marmot just looked on. Then they all lay down and went to sleep and the young marmot was alone.

He had nobody to play with and nobody to talk to, which he thought was unfair. In the end, he kept repeating to himself, "I'm not going to sleep, I'm not." Then he yawned and soon after he fell fast asleep with the rest of his family.

Santa and the Police

It was the 24th December and Santa Claus was in a great hurry. He whizzed along the streets on his sleigh laden with presents of all shapes and sizes, and thought to himself, "What a good job I've got the new engine for my sleigh. It means I can get along a lot faster. I won't need to use the reindeer this year. Rudolph and his friends can have a holiday this Christmas." Then Santa parked his sleigh at the roadside and carried his big sack into a large block of flats where lots of children lived. When he returned to his sleigh, half an hour later, after delivering all the presents, he saw a policeman inspecting the sleigh.

"Good evening," called Santa Claus and was about to get back into the sleigh when the policeman said, "Just a minute, young man, you have parked on a double yellow line." Then he broke off in mid-sentence when he realised he was talking to Santa Claus!
"Oh, I'm terribly sorry, Sir, I didn't realise it was you, Mr Santa Claus," said the policeman.

So, Santa went on his way delivering presents, whilst the policeman thought to himself, "Now I understand why he had no number plate."

The Woodpecker

"I say," said the squirrel to the woodpecker. "Why do you make such a racket, tapping on the tree trunk? The other birds don't make nearly so much noise as you." "God gave me a very long beak so I can tap against the tree trunk and fish out all the beetles and caterpillars that are there," replied the woodpecker.

"Oh I didn't realise that," said the squirrel. "Besides, have you never thought how useful I am for the trees because I rid them of all kinds of dangerous insects which live under their bark?" replied the woodpecker.

This made the squirrel go very quiet and he said, "I'll never say anything against your tapping again now I know all the facts." Then the squirrel went on his way to find some food for lunch.

The Sleepwalker

Whenever the moon was full Carol would get up and wander around the house in her nightdress.

One night Carol was sleepwalking when she met her mother on the stairs who asked, "Where are you off to, little sleepwalker?" "I must find a star for my Mummy," replied Carol. "Leave the star in the sky and go back to bed," replied her mother, trying to reassure her daughter as she led her back to bed.

Since then her mother has always made sure that Carol's bedroom curtains have been drawn properly when there's a full moon.

Carol has not walked in her sleep since her mother put up some thick curtains at her window. These keep the room dark even when there is a full moon.

The Raven 1

Clive loved his grandfather very much. His grandfather knew the answers to his questions and he talked to people, animals and even to plants!

He said to Clive, "Everything that is alive speaks a language — and if you listen very carefully you can hear it. I do not just talk to the animals and plants but I take care of them as well, and they are very grateful."

Clive did not really understand what his grandfather meant, but some time later he had a special experience with an animal and learnt a lot from it.

One sunny morning, Clive was woken up by a bird screeching. He got up, went outside and found a big, black raven sitting on the windowsill. Clive began to talk to the bird as his grandfather had suggested. Clive asked the raven lots of questions. "Where are you from? What's the matter? Can I help you?"

The raven just stared blankly at him as Clive got closer and closer. He got so near that he could almost stroke the bird. Then a noise from the house scared the bird and it tried to fly off but could not because it had a damaged wing. Clive went up to the bird and said, "I'll take care of you until you're able to fly again."

The Raven 2

What a pity that Grandad had gone away for a few days, just when Clive could have done with his advice. He read through his book on birds and noted that ravens eat insects, snails and worms.

Immediately after breakfast Clive went out to search for insects and worms for his raven. Eventually he had caught three worms, seven flies and two snails and he put this pile of food in the hedge for the raven. That evening just before he went to bed Clive visited the hedge and saw that the raven had eaten all the food. Then he said to the bird, "Don't fly off, little raven, I'll help you. I'll bring you food every day until you're well again."

So from then on Clive searched for worms and insects every day before he went to school and took them to the raven, and chatted to the bird for a little while.

The Raven 3

One morning Clive woke up when he heard the raven squawking. He looked outside and sure enough, his raven was sitting on the window ledge.

"How are you then?" asked Clive and noticed that the wing was now mended. He realised that his raven was now well enough to fly, but Clive hoped that the bird would not leave because he had grown very fond of him.

But this was not to be. The raven then stretched its wings and flew up into the sky, leaving Clive feeling very lonely.

Later that day, Grandfather came back from his journey and Clive was able to tell him all about his raven. "You must be patient," said Clive's grandfather, "animals have their own way of thanking you."

A few days later, when Clive was coming home from school he heard a familiar screech coming from the garden and saw the raven flying towards him. Then his friend landed on his shoulder.

From that day on the raven accompanied Clive to school. His friends could not understand that you had to talk to an animal and care for it before you could win its friendship and trust.

The Riddle

Mark loved riddles and made up lots of them every day. "What's this?" he said to his mother. "You can read it and it has four wheels." His mother thought it over and said, "Is it a book?" "No, that does not have four wheels," replied Mark.

"You can climb into this thing and then read," explained Mark. "It gets odder and odder," said his mother. "Is it a car?" she suggested. "Yes, but what kind of car?" asked Mark.

"Oh, I give up, you'll have to tell me," said his mother. "It's the mobile library that comes to the village once a week. People climb into it and choose books to read!" exclaimed Mark. He was very proud of himself for thinking up such a good riddle all by himself.

The New Clock

Sandra was sitting doing her homework in her father's study. A new clock hung on the wall which looked very different from the others she had seen. This new clock had no numbers, only dashes on its face.

"Sandra!" called her mother from the kitchen, "my kitchen clock has stopped, please can you tell me the right time." "Err, it's mmm . . . eleven minutes to eight," said Sandra, guessing because she could not tell the time properly on this clock.

"No, it can't be that, it must be eleven minutes past eight!" replied her mother.

"Oh, Mummy, I like clocks with numbers far more than this one with dashes," said Sandra, blaming the new clock because she had not learnt how to tell the time properly.

Santa has a Rest

"It's time for a rest," said Santa Claus and sat down on his sledge. "I feel absolutely worn out. I know that most people think that I just work on one day of the year, but that is not true at all. I have to be well prepared for Christmas. I have to make up thousands of parcels, check my lists, oil the sledge, tend to the reindeer and see to the little helpers, and so on," said Santa Claus to himself.

"So I must say in all honesty that I am an extremely busy man. I'm not complaining because it's all made worthwhile when I see the happy faces and shining eyes of the children opening their presents on Christmas morning.

"Now I'd better get back to work and start giving out the presents or there won't be any happy faces this year!" said Santa Claus, laughing to himself as he loaded up the sledge.

The Animals' Party

"We're holding a party," said the nightingale.

"What shall we eat?" asked the blue-tits.

"Apple strudel," shouted the poodle.

"What shall we have to drink?" asked the finch.

"Wine!" grunted the pig.

"We want to dance," squeaked the mice.

"The blackbirds will play the flute!" croaked the frogs.

"How long will it go on for?" hissed the snake.

"Until midnight," howled the wolves.

"But where?" asked the flea.

"In the forester's house," mewed the cat. And with that the meeting ended.

The Telephone Gnome

The Dixon family are a very normal family. They live in a small house, have two children, a car and a dog.

But they have a telephone gnome which means they are not quite normal. This mischievous gnome lives in the telephone receiver and creates havoc all day long.

He makes the telephone ring and when someone answers it, he giggles and shouts out stupid things. Sometimes he blows down the telephone or he whistles down it. He has even spoken on behalf of Mr Dixon, ordering things such as a huge chocolate cake and a new vacuum cleaner.

The family finally ran out of patience with him, and thought up schemes to get rid of him. "We should ask the firemen to come and spray water down the receiver," suggested Jane. "We should go on holiday," said Mrs Dixon, "but we can't because it is still term time."

"I know what we'll do," said Mr Dixon. "We'll take the phone off the hook for a while. Then the gnome will get bored and go away!" And that's just what they did.

The whole family were overjoyed at the peace that reigned in the house when the gnome left. It got very bored because it could not get up to its naughty tricks with the telephone off the hook. The Dixons all heaved a sigh of relief and said, "Thank goodness he's gone. Now we can have a bit of peace and quiet at long last."

The Robin has a Bath

Have you ever seen a robin having a bath? He does not need soap or a sponge or a towel, like we do.

Instead he flies to the stream in the early morning and sits down on a stone. Then he dives in and out of the water. Next he shakes out the drops of water from his feathers and twirls round and round. After that he combs his feathers out with his little beak. Then he dries himself in the warm sun which is much more pleasant than using a towel.

Afterwards he soars up into the blue sky and catches three fat juicy flies for breakfast.

Clearing Up the Cellar

It was a rainy November day and Michael was bored. He had read all his favourite books and played with all his toys. Then he was looking for something to do.

"You would be doing me a big favour," said his mother, "if you cleared up the cellar." Michael agreed to do this and went down into the cellar. He began to clear up the bottles and boxes and generally tidied up the clutter. His mother could hear him hard at work for a while, then it went quiet. So she crept down into the cellar to see what was happening. And what did she see there?

Michael was sitting on the floor playing with some old toys that he had found in the cellar. They were toys he had played with as a baby. Michael had blown the trumpet, filled a wooden lorry with blocks and played with a jigsaw.

He did not notice his mother come into the cellar because he was so involved with his old toys. She went back upstairs because she did not want to disturb him.

The Good Spirit

The good spirits of the fire live in the fireplaces of large houses in Russia, and you can still find them there to this very day.

In one farmhouse in particular, the whole family sits down above the fireplace when it is very cold outside and warm themselves from the fire. There is no central heating in this particular farmhouse.

For months on end when there is deep snow outside and the temperature is well below freezing, the family will sit above the fireplace and be cosy and snug. It can be so cold in Russia during the Winter that even the windows get covered in a thick layer of ice. When it gets very cold outside the whole family sleeps above the fireplace.

So, as you can see, it is vital that the fire is never allowed to go out. The good spirits that live in the grate of the fire see to it that the fire never goes out. In this home, the Grandmother takes care of the fire and of the good spirits. She treats the spirits well and is very kind to them.

Just before the children go to bed in the evening the Grandmother stokes up the fire and puts on a pan of soup to heat over the flames so that it will be ready the next day. She talks to the spirits in the grate for several minutes. Then the flames dance and whilst the whole household sleeps, the spirits keep the fire alive until the morning.

back through the workshop into the house and up the stairs to his bedroom. Now his mother understood why there were always black footprints on the carpet and on his sheets — Jim walked across the dirty workshop floor in his bare feet to get to the beloved tractor!

The Soap Bubbles

Rebecca has been given a "Bubbles" set for her birthday. So now she can blow lots of bubbles. She takes off the lid and pulls out a ring and dips the ring in the soapy water, and then blows through the ring to make lots of bubbles.

Rebecca blows and blows and soon she has made lots of bubbles. Some of the soap bubbles go as high as the clouds. Another bubble floats down into a children's playground and when a child makes a grab for it, it bursts. So you see a bubble does not have a very long life.

The Footprints

Jim was five years old and loved machines and motor cars more than anything else in the world. That's not surprising, as his father owns a garage repair business, which deals mainly in tractors and combine harvesters.

Several days ago a brand new tractor was delivered to the work shop and Jim spent every spare minute with it. He sat on it, and pretended to be a tractor driver.

His mother was very concerned about the black footprints she saw every morning on Jim's bed sheets and on his bedroom carpet. Where did they come from? Jim has a bath every night! So she decided to investigate the matter further.

When she had put Jim to bed one night, she left the room as usual. Then she waited downstairs in the hall.

It was not long before Jim crept out of his bedroom in his pyjamas, and went down the stairs, barefoot! Then he went through the work shop to see the new tractor. He jumped up onto the tractor seat and pretended to be a tractor driver going along a farm track.

After a while he jumped down and crept

Rosa in the Wood

Rosa, the witch, and her apprentice, Max, were walking through the forest one day collecting weeds and herbs. "Pss," hissed Rosa tugging at Max's sleeve. "Look over there!" Max did as she said and saw a family having a picnic at the edge of the wood.

"I've seen these people before," said the witch. "They often come here for a picnic and then leave all their rubbish behind when they go. Let's teach them a lesson so that they'll never leave their litter behind in the forest again."

So Rosa and Max crept up to where the family was sitting. When they reached the car, they stopped. Rosa said the magic words, "Snake's tongue, and wasp's sting open the car boot!"

Hey presto, the boot opened and Rosa emptied the contents of a litter bin into it. Soon the boot was filled with tin cans, bottles, plastic cups, banana skins, apple cores and cigarette ends. "That looks awful!" exclaimed Max. They were both well pleased with their work. When they had closed the boot they hid behind a bush to wait for the family to finish the picnic and open the boot.

It was not long before the family finished their picnic, but instead of opening the boot, they just got into the car and drove home. "They're in for a big surprise when they open the boot," said Rosa gleefully to Max.

The Hedgehog

One day in Autumn the hedgehog met up with a cat. The cat said, "I've been watching you for ages and you just eat and eat but you're never ill. I eat a lot but I could never eat as much as you!"

"I'm stocking up," replied the hedgehog.

"What for?" asked the cat.

"Haven't you heard of a Winter sleep?" replied the hedgehog.

"I eat and get fat now, then I have enough food to live off during the Winter when I'm asleep," explained the hedgehog.

"Gosh!" exclaimed the cat, "you can go for such a long time without food? You must be really hungry by Spring!"

"That's right," answered the hedgehog. "Come and see me in the Spring and we'll chat again."

The Thin Hedgehog

As agreed, the cat and the hedgehog met again the following Spring. "Good heavens," exclaimed the cat, "you're as thin as a rake!"

"That's not surprising," answered the hedgehog, "I've just woken up after one hundred and thirty four days asleep."

"Your tummy is really thin and your prickles look weak and limp, you look really wretched," said the cat.

"I'm absolutely starving," said the hedgehog "Don't delay me any longer. I must find some food!" said the hedgehog to the cat, and set off in search of food. Soon he found a big fat juicy worm and some beetles. He gobbled them up at once. By the evening he felt much better and in a few days he was sure that he would be back to his usual fat self!

The Rocking Chair

Back and forth! It was good fun in Grandfather's rocking chair. Bill thought it great to rock to and fro, to and fro, faster and faster! He didn't hear his Grandmother as she said, "Be careful or you'll topple over in the chair!"

Faster and faster, he rocked until both he and the rocking chair jumped out of the window onto the street. They bumped into a policeman controlling the traffic and said, "Do you want to come with us?" and the policeman landed in his lap.

And off they went again picking up two pigs as they journeyed along. This mad rocking chair journey went on until it reached the lake and then wham! Bill fell into the pond. Brrr . . . it was cold. Then next thing he knew his Grandmother was washing his face with a flannel.

"You've got a big lump on your head," she said, "and all because you would not listen to me." "Oh, Grandma," whined Bill, "you've spoilt my journey. Where are all the others now?" "It was all a dream. You fell off the chair and passed out for a while. You're lucky, you've only got a slight bump on your head," said Grandma. "It could have been much worse."

He reached up and felt his head and sure enough he had a lump, but the memory of his wonderful journey eased the pain.

The Poor Calendar

"Oh dear!" sighed the calendar one December day. "I'm getting thinner and thinner every day, and feeling weaker and weaker. I think I've come to the end. I was fat and healthy at the start of the year, but now, there are only a few pages left of me. Oh dear!"

Soon, a new, fat calendar was hung up next to the old one. "Ooh you are thin and bedraggled," said the new one disdainfully. "Look at me, don't I look good!"

"Oh you'll soon be like me. You wait until this time next year, and then you'll look just like me," answered the thin one. "That's the way it goes!"

The new calendar was very thoughtful. He wondered if what the calendar said was true. One thing was for sure, time would tell!

The Guessing Game

"Guess where I've been," said Charles, standing on the doorstep, to his mother one day. "You've been down to the building site. It is fairly obvious. I can tell that from the sand on your boots, the earth on your trousers and the bits of cement on your jacket," replied his mother.

A few days later Charles asked his mother again to guess where he had been. "This time it is obvious that you have been in the wood. I can tell from the pine needles in your hair and the mud on your hands," she said to Charles who was standing on the doorstep.

The next time Charles decided to cheat so that his mother would not be able to guess where he had been. He crept out of the house, rang the doorbell and asked innocently from the doorstep, "Guess where I've been?"

His mother burst out laughing when she heard her son say this and answered, "It's obvious where you have been — you've just come from the larder and not from outdoors because you've got cream all round your mouth! You little rascal!"

The New Baby

John was overjoyed to see his mother again. She had been in hospital for over a week to have a new baby. John had really missed her.

He also wanted to know the answers to lots of questions such as, "Can fish speak?" "What do angels eat in heaven?" "Have I got a little brother? . . ."

When John's mother returned home with the new baby she gave John a big hug. Then she made him sit down and she placed the new born baby in his lap. She said, "This is your new little sister. I hope you'll help to look after her."

John went very quiet and touched the baby's tiny hands and nose. He soon forgot all the questions he wanted to ask his Mummy because he was so pleased to have a little sister.

Bill and Ben

"Hey, Bill, how did you come to have such a big bump on your head?" asked his friend.

"Oh I did it in a car accident. I went for a ride in my uncle's car and I forgot to fasten my safety belt. Then when my uncle had to put on his brakes suddenly, I was thrown against the windscreen!" explained Bill.

"Goodness!" exclaimed Ben. "It sounds as though you were lucky to get away with such a minor injury. It could have been much more serious. But you were really silly not to wear your safety belt! I always put mine on, besides it is against the law not to wear a seat belt. Better make sure you wear yours from now on!"

"Don't worry," said Bill, "I'll always wear my seat belt in the future. I learnt my lesson the hard way!"

Rosa

Rosa set off for the witches' meeting that was to take place far away on the top of a mountain. She prepared herself for the long journey and got out her magic chair. She put a soft cushion on it to make her journey more comfortable. She said goodbye to Max, her apprentice, and set off on the magic chair which would fly her to the meeting.

Max went inside to clean up the kitchen and to put away the broken broom. He had done most of the tidying up, when he heard a strange sound coming from outside the cottage. He went out and saw Rosa and her chair. "You're back early!" exclaimed Max. "I was not expecting you for another two hours."

"I did not expect to be back so soon," said Rosa. "But the other witches all laughed at my flying chair. They are not at all interested in new and different ideas. So I left before the meeting started. Besides those meetings are so boring that I won't have missed much. From now on, I'm stopping here where I belong! Meetings are a waste of my valuable time. Now, let's get to work and make up some new magic potions." And with that Rosa and Max began to look up some new spells in the Book of Spells.

The Trick Egg

Julia made up a new game. She called it her Sunday Breakfast Egg Trick. First of all she ate her boiled egg and then she turned it upside down in the egg cup so that it looked just like an uneaten, boiled egg.

"Here you are, Daddy, your egg is ready now!" said Julia to her father, quite innocently handing him the boiled egg. Her father thanked her and then he hit the egg shell with his spoon to remove the shell and get at the egg. Then he looked shocked — the egg he had been looking forward to, had already been eaten!

Julia particularly enjoyed playing this trick on visitors who were new to the game. Because they were the most surprised of all!

Mr Mole

Mr Mole lived under the ground. He had dug out his home all by himself using his paws and he had even laid a moss carpet on the floor.

So, as you can see, he is a busy fellow. Instead of just settling down in his new home, Mr Mole carried on digging out more tunnels. He has very poor eyesight and can barely tell the difference between light and dark.

Sometimes he surfaces above ground to throw out the earth. You can see his little hills all over the meadows and sometimes even in gardens. When Mr Mole leaves a mound of earth on a smooth green lawn, the owner is not at all pleased.

The farmers on the other hand, say, "I know that the mole is very useful because he eats lots of bugs and grubs but all those hills make haymaking very difficult indeed." If only Mr Mole did not dig so much and had a rest now and again!

The Thorn Bush

When Jesus was captured in Jerusalem, a boy was sent out to find a crown of thorns. He found a thorn bush and plucked a few branches from it. When the bush knew what the branches were going to be used for it was very troubled.

When Jesus rose from the dead on Easter Day and went through the gardens blessing all the flowers and bushes, he went up to the thorn bush and asked, "Why do you look so bare and wintry." "Oh, Jesus, how can I bloom knowing that the thorns from my branches scratched you and made you bleed."

Jesus was very touched by what the bush said, and gave it a white blossom as a sign of its innocence. Since then the thorn bush has always bloomed at Easter time.

Impractical Grandad!

"My father, who was your Grandfather," said Aunt Lottie to her nephew, "was a very clever man but not very practical. He was not like modern men of today, who help to bring up their children and cook, and do all the other things around the home. No he was very different, very old fashioned. I remember a funny story which happened when I was a young girl."

One day I went with my father on a long train journey. I was four years old at the time and we were going to spend a few weeks at my aunt's house because my mother was expecting another baby, and so she wanted me out of the way.

Because the journey took so long, I went to sleep after first taking off my shoes. When we arrived at our destination it was already dark outside. My father hurriedly put on my shoes for me and we got off the train.

We still had quite a long way to walk to my aunt's house. "My feet are killing me," I moaned after a few steps. "Just try to keep up with me," answered my father sharply. But it was not long before I started to complain again, and then I asked to be carried. But my father had two heavy cases to carry and so he could not possibly carry me as well. He encouraged me to try to walk a little further because we were nearly at Aunt Joan's house.

It seemed an eternity before we reached the house. When we arrived at the house my aunt was waiting to greet us. "Here you are, at long last!" she said. I said, "Hello, Aunt Joan, my feet are killing me!" Then she looked down at my feet and saw that my father hd put my shoes on the wrong way round! My father was such a well-meaning fellow but so impractical!

Eric, the Dream Pilot

Eric and his father were making a model of an aeroplane from a kit. The two of them were having a conversation about aeroplanes and pilots.

Eric's father is a pilot and it is clear that Eric also wants to be one when he grows up! "A pilot has to know all the parts of his plane," said Eric's father. "But, aren't there mechanics who look after the plane and its engine?" asked Eric.

"There are, but the pilot needs to know what to do in an emergency. He needs to pass lots of difficult examinations before he is allowed to fly alone," explained Eric's father.

"You must have passed all the exams then, Dad," said Eric. "Yes I did," said his father, "but I had to swot hard and spend hours doing extra homework. If you want to be a pilot you'll have to stop complaining about the amount of homework you get."

Eric thought the conversation was becoming rather tiresome now and decided it was time for a change. So he said, "I think tea's ready now." During tea, Eric thought to himself, "What a pity I need to pass so many exams to be a pilot! I'll show them that I can be a good pilot. I will make emergency landings in the middle of the desert without passing all the stupid exams!"

The Guessing Game

John has a riddle for his brother and sister. They have to guess what he is describing.

"The machine starts up very sluggishly. Soon the big tyres start to go round. They have huge tracks on them. Next it moves forwards slowly, then it puts its great mouth into the earth and starts to dig up shovelfuls of clay. When its mouth is full it moves its gigantic arm to the side and empties the earth into a waiting lorry."

"Haven't you guessed what I'm describing by now, or have you two never seen a building site?" John asks his puzzled brother and sister.

The Turkish Neighbours

"I'm going next door to give them a piece of my mind for dumping that rubbish in the garden," said Steven. Shortly afterwards he went round and knocked at the house next door, where a Turkish family called Gediktasch lived.

A man with a black moustache and brown skin answered the door. Behind him stood a toddler. "What you want?" asked Mr Gediktasch. "Listen here . . ." began Steven, but the Turkish man held out his hand and said, "I Mustafa, you come in, my wife makes Turkish coffee."

Steven was ushered into a very comfortable room and invited to sit down. As he looked around the room he was amazed how clean and tidy it was. Far tidier than he had imagined it would be.

Then the little Turkish boy sat on his knee and although Steven could not understand a word he was saying, he found the little boy very friendly. Soon after Mrs Gediktasch brought in the coffee and they all began to drink it.

But Steven still had not mentioned the rubbish. Just as he was about to say something about it Mustafa said, "Lot of rubbish left here. Why people do that? I do not know where to put rubbish." Steven smiled as he heard this and suggested that he took the rubbish to the tip with Mustafa next Saturday. "What nice people they are after all," thought Steven as he returned home.

The Skiing Accident

The accident would never have happened if Anna had not been so brave, and if the other children had been more sensible.

One sunny Winter's day, Anna and her friends went skiing. The boys had made a small jump. They jumped over it like real ski jumpers! Only Anna was scared to jump it! The slope was too steep for her.

But the other children kept telling her to have a go and said, "Don't be such a coward, go on, have a go at the jump, it's easy!" In the end Anna thought to herself, "I'll show them I'm no coward! I'll try that ski jump."

Then she took a deep breath and skied towards the jump. She cleared the jump easily, too easily in fact, and she landed in some very deep snow. She looked so funny, stuck in the snow with her skis pointing upwards, that all the others burst out laughing. When Anna tried to stand up they stopped laughing though.

They tried to help her up, but she just screamed out in pain! In the end she had to be taken in an ambulance to the hospital. "It's a broken ankle," said the doctor, "how did it happen?" Anna knew, and the other children knew, exactly how it had happened, and how it need never have happened.

The Twelve Brothers

Twelve brothers were standing at the door at New Year. The first one said, "I bring the cold, frost and snow." The second one said, "I'm the smallest, but perhaps the jolliest." The third one said, "I bring the first snowdrops and the Easter eggs." The fourth one said, "I bring the Spring."

The fifth one said, "Everybody loves me, because I wear a garland of flowers in my hair." The sixth one said, "I ripen the cherries and warm the nights." The seventh one said, "I bring the Summer, the harvest and holidays!" The eighth one said, "I'm often hot and stormy."

The ninth one said, "I bring ripe apples, and kites in the sky." The tenth one said, "I blow the leaves from the trees." The eleventh one said, "I bring the fog and cosy evenings by the fire."

The twelfth one said, "I am by far the best — I bring Christmas cheer and the sparkle in the children's eyes." Do you know who the twelve brothers are?

The Knitting Needles

There was once a poor old lady who went into the forest to collect some wood. She saw a kitten lying in the hedge and felt sorry for it. She took it back to her tiny cottage and gave it some milk to drink. Soon the kitten was well and one day ran off.

Sometime later the old lady went into the forest again to collect some wood. And this time, to her astonishment she saw a lady winking at her from the same spot where she had found the kitten. When the old lady went nearer the hedge, the strange lady threw her a pair of knitting needles, and then vanished.

The poor old lady returned home and, leaving the knitting needles on the table, she went to bed. The next morning when she went downstairs she was puzzled when she found a pair of socks had been knitted and now lay on the table.

The next evening the old lady left the knitting needles on the table again, and the next day she found another pair of socks had been knitted during the night.

The old lady realised that she had been given a pair of magic knitting needles as a reward for taking care of the sick kitten.

From then on, the poor old lady led a comfortable life, selling the pairs of socks.

Sneezing

"Hey, Bill!" called Ben. "Let's go for a walk!" "Atischooo!" replied Bill, sneezing. "I say, I need an umbrella if you're going to start sneezing like that, haven't you got a handkerchief? I don't want to catch your germs," said Ben.

"Of course, I've got a handkerchief. Look, it is a spotted one!" answered Bill. "Well hold it in front of your mouth and nose when you sneeze in future," said Ben.

"Oh, I've only got a bit of a cold. It's nothing to get upset about, you won't catch it," said Bill. "I might catch the virus that caused the cold though," said Ben thoughtfully.

"I think I'll go for a walk by myself, you really ought to be in bed with that cold." And with that Ben set off for a walk on his own.

The Beggar

"Mummy," said the child, "there is a man outside asking for charity." The mother went to have a look for herself, and found an old, shabbily dressed man standing in the doorway.

He said, "Good lady, please give me something, a little money perhaps." The mother felt sorry for the beggar and gave him a few coins.

The beggar thanked her politely and then went on his way. "The man wanted some money," explained the child's mother, "charity used to be a virtue but it has a different meaning these days!"

The Christmas Tree

Christmas Eve was always the same at the Borg household. When the clock struck midnight, they would open the lounge door and sing, 'Silent night. . . .' Then the children would unwrap their presents.

The whole family sang, in front of the tree. They all marvelled at the twinkling lights. Nobody noticed Laura creep under the tree to put her brand new shoes on which gleamed almost as much as the lights on the tree.

"Oh Laura," said her mother, "how can you be so vain when you're only three years old!"

The Matches

"Hey, Bill!" called Ben. "Look what I've brought you for your birthday!" "Gosh, a box of matches, now I can light my own candles on the cake," said Bill.

"Yes, they're really good matches, I've tried them out already," added Ben.

"Oh no!" cried Bill. "Then they aren't any use if you've struck them!"

"Oh but Bill, in that case," said Ben, "they're just the right present for you. They will stop you getting into mischief!"

The Birch Rod

Mother always kept a birch rod out of sight behind the cupboard. She used it on very rare occasions when her children were especially naughty. Mother wanted us to know the difference between right and wrong.

She once used it on Walter when he had been playing with matches in bed and very nearly set the whole house on fire! She also used it once on Jason when he refused to get up to go to school. His excuse was that he felt ill and he was fed up with going to school every day.

She even used it on me when I told one of my mother's friends that I had lice in my hair! She was furious with me for saying that!

Indeed, my mother had cause to use the birch rod when she did! What surprises me most, is that she did not use it more often!

Riddles!

"Hey, Bill!" called Ben. "Let's play at making up riddles." "Alright then, you begin because I can't think of any just now," replied Bill.

"Right then, what is this — it is on a roof smoking a packet of cigarettes?" said Ben. "Oh, I know that, it's simple, it must be a roof builder," answered Bill. "Wrong," said Ben, "it is a chimney!"

"Next one, what creeps into a hole and leaves its tail outside?" asked Ben. "I know," said Bill, "a mouse?" "Wrong again, it is a cat! If a mouse left its tail outside the hole, then the cat would catch it," replied Ben.

"Another one, — it hangs on the wall and ticks, and when it falls the clock breaks!" said Bill. "Ha, ha," said Ben, "you have just given the riddle away."

Cooking is Fun

The two boys decided to bake a cake for their mother as it was her birthday the following day. When she went shopping that afternoon, the boys set to work.

They decided to make a fruit cake. They mixed together flour, butter, eggs and sugar in the mixing bowl. Then they poured the mixture into a cake tin and because there was no more room on the kitchen table, Jonathan put the cake tin on a stool. He only had to add the fruit and then the cake could go in the oven.

Paul was getting a little tired and as he remarked to his brother, "Cooking is fun, isn't it, Jonathan?" he sat down on the stool! "Don't sit there!" called Jonathan, but it was too late, Paul had sat right on the cake tin.

When he got up from the stool, there was cake mixture all over the back of his pants! "Quick take off your trousers and wash them whilst I make another cake. I think we have just enough time before Mummy gets back," said Jonathan.

David and the Dentist

David woke up in the middle of the night with terrible toothache. His cheek was swollen. His mother put a bandage soaked in camomile over his cheek, to get the swelling down.

"Tomorrow morning, we're going straight to the dentist," said his mother. So the next morning she took David to the dentist.

David hated going to the dentist. Whilst sitting in the waiting-room he suddenly announced, "Oh Mummy, the pain has gone now, let's go home." David did not really mean this because his tooth was hurting him a lot. He was just scared of seeing the dentist.

David was out of luck as the receptionist called, "Next please!" David had to see the dentist. He examined David's teeth and decided that one of his teeth, the one that was hurting, needed filling.

No sooner said than done. The dentist was drilling away in no time! When it was all over, and the tooth was filled, David felt very relieved and wondered why he had made such a fuss about going to the dentist in the past. From then on he quite enjoyed going.

The Mice and the Cats

One day the mice decided to hold a big meeting. "Friends," said Chairman Mouse, "this can't go on any longer. The cats are getting more daring and we are living in fear of losing our lives! We must do something!"

"Quite right," called the other mice, "we really must do something but what?"

"We could set up sentry posts to warn us when the cats are coming near," suggested one mouse. But the others thought that this idea sounded too much like hard work.

"We could hang a bell around the cats' necks so that we will hear them coming," suggested one young mouse. The other mice thought this was a great idea, until the Chairman asked, "Who will hang the bells around their necks?"

At that, all the mice became very quiet, and nobody volunteered to hang the bells on the cats. In the end the meeting broke up with the mice not reaching a firm decision! Life would carry on as before for the mice.

The Proud Apple

There was once a red apple that was far more beautiful than all the other apples on the tree. One day this apple said, "I won't be shaken or picked like the others, for I will stay on the tree forever so that everyone can admire me!"

When the harvest began, people started to pick all the apples but the red one stayed on the tree. At the end of harvesting only the red apple was still left on the tree.

The red apple thoroughly enjoyed the last days of Summer and thought to itself, "This is great! All the others have been peeled and eaten or stored away! How awful for them!"

Then Autumn came, and the wind blew hard and the proud, red apple became wrinkled and shrivelled.

One day the apple fell from the branch onto the hard earth below, and it yearned to be one of the other apples that were stored in the cellar! But it was too late for that now . . . the red apple should not have been so proud.

Going Visiting

"Hey Ben," said Bill to his friend, "today we're going to Grandma's." "Yippee!" yelled Ben. "Quick, let's go then."

"Hang on a minute," said Bill, "your fingernails are filthy. You had better scrub them clean before we set off for Grandma's." "Oh but Bill," said Ben, "Grandma has such poor eyesight she won't notice my dirty fingernails."

"I absolutely insist that you clean them first and then we'll go to Grandma's," said Bill. So Ben had no alternative but to scrub his fingernails clean.

The Rainbow

When it stopped raining the sun shone again and a wonderful seven-coloured rainbow spanned across the sky.

"Isn't that beautiful!" cried the twins. This was the first time they had seen a rainbow. "How do you get rainbows?" asked the twins.

Their elder brother replied, "Don't you know? Then go and look for yourselves, where the rainbow begins you'll find seven pots of paint!"

The twins set off in search of the paint pots, meanwhile the mother said to the boy, "How can you be so mean? You've told them such a pack of lies. They'll be so disappointed when they come back. Do you really know how you get rainbows?" The boy admitted that he did not really know how rainbows are made.

The Recorder

"Robert, have you practised the recorder today?" asked his mother for the fifth time. She always got the reply, "I'll do it later."

Then one day Robert had a brilliant idea. He played the recorder onto his tape and every day he would play it back so that his mother thought he was practising.

This went on for a long time and Robert's mother was satisfied. Until yesterday, when she went into his room and saw Robert lying flat out on his bed, reading a book whilst the tape recorder was playing! From then on Robert practised the recorder every day.

The Shower

It was the third time in a week that Kevin had appeared at the front door completely covered in mud. "You're not coming into the house like that," said his mother, pushing him out of the door. "But Mummy, everybody will see me standing here!" said Kevin. His mother gave in and said, "Alright then, come in, but don't you dare get covered in mud again."

A few days later Kevin appeared at the door looking as though he had been dragged through a hedge backwards. His mother took off his wellington boots and led him to the bathroom. Then she put him under the shower, in his trousers, shirt and jumper.

"Now, you and your clothes will be washed in one go!" said his mother. "I'm warning you, next time I'll put you and your clothes into the washing machine together, how would you like that?" To this day however, she has never carried out this final threat!

The White Stag

There were once three hunters who wanted to kill the rare white stag. Although they had never seen him, they had heard a lot about him.

When they were in the forest one day, they decided to have a rest and they lay down under a tree and fell asleep. When they woke up, the first hunter said, "I dreamt that the white stag jumped out of the bush!" The second hunter said, "I dreamt that we went after him and I shot him." Then the third said, "I dreamt that I blew the horn to signal the end of the hunt!"

And as the three hunters lay talking, the white stag trotted past them. Although they jumped up and grabbed their rifles when they realised it was the rare white stag, they had no hope of catching up with it because it was already miles away!

The Trader and his Son

There was once a rich trader whose only son longed to travel. The son wanted to see something of the world, before he took over his father's business.

He went on his travels and his father heard nothing from his son for a long time.

Then the rich trader became very ill and knew he was soon to die. He called his best friend to him and said, "Search for my son throughout the land, he is to inherit my estate. I am leaving everything to him." Then the rich trader died.

The friend searched everywhere and eventually found three men who claimed to be the trader's son. The friend set up a picture of the trader and said that whoever hit the trader's heart with an arrow would be the true and rightful heir.

The first one took up his bow and aimed, but he hit the shoulder. The second one hit the trader's neck. Then the third one took up his bow but he put it down and said, "I can't pierce my father's heart."

When the friend heard this he knew that the third one was the trader's true son and rightful heir.

187

The Little Train

A little black steam train chugged its way through Toytown. When it had to pull lots of heavy wagons it hissed, "Puff, puff this is hard work!"

And when it went up hill it puffed even more and said, "Help me! Help me!" When it finally reached the top it said, "At last I've made it! Phew!"

Then when it went down hill again, it spluttered, "This is good, this is easy!" If you go to Toytown you will see the little black train.

Fire! Fire!

One afternoon when Caroline was sitting in her room reading, she suddenly heard someone shout, "Fire!" She rushed over to the window but she could not see any sign of the fire, so she went back to her book.

Then she heard the fire engine and called out, "Where is the fire then?" She ran into the living room where her brother was watching a film on television.

"There's a fire on this programme," he said laughing. Then their mother added, "Don't worry, Caroline, I once went to answer our telephone when it was one on the television that was ringing."

Jumbo and Pipsi

Jumbo, the elephant, and Pipsi, the mouse, were great pals. When they were going for a walk one day, Jumbo stood on his tiny friend's toes accidentally. "Oh, I'm so sorry," he apologised.

"That's alright," said Pipsi, "no need to apologise."

One day when the two of them went for a swim, Jumbo was in the water long before Pipsi, who was searching for his trunks on the beach. "Hey, Jumbo, have you put my trunks on by mistake? I can't find them anywhere," called Pipsi. "No, I haven't got them on — chance would be a fine thing!" replied Jumbo.

Mitsu

The little Japanese girl Mitsu, spends almost every day in her parents' garden. Although she has no brothers or sisters and no toys she is happy and contented. The splendid flowers and shrubs, the little bridges and the pool make her happy.

Japanese gardens are very well cared for and famed throughout the world for their beauty. When the little Mitsu wandered through the garden, she would always find something new to look at. She would sing as she went through the garden and all the birds would listen to her clear voice.

She would always carry her little casket around with her which held a chirping cricket. Mitsu liked to hear her cricket chirp and she loved him dearly.

In the very bottom of the casket were some beautiful pearls. They shone and gleamed like a starry sky. Mitsu's grandmother said, "Pearls are the mermaid's tears."

Mitsu then decided to open up the casket and leave it on the windowsill so that the mermaids would come, when the moon was full, and she could give them back their tears. Then they would be as happy as she was.

Shopping!

"Mummy, I've been invited to Mary's birthday party!" called Angela as she came in from school. "That will be nice for you," said her mother, "but can you go shopping for me and buy me a bag of flour, a tube of mustard and a bottle of lemonade. Do you want me to write that down for you or can you remember it all?"

Angela replied disdainfully, "I'm not a baby, of course I can remember all that." As she wandered along to the shops, her thoughts were on Mary's party — what should she buy her? What would there be to eat?

When she went into the shop she asked the shopkeeper for a tube of flour, a bottle of mustard and a bag of lemonade! The shopkeeper roared with laughter.

"No, I err . . . mean," stuttered Angela, "a bottle of flour, a tube of lemonade and a bag of mustard!" Then the shopkeeper laughed again, and said, "I think you're miles away today! But wait, I know what your mother wants — a bag of flour, a tube of mustard and a bottle of lemonade. That's right isn't it?"

"Yes," replied Angela red in the face, but glad that the shopkeeper was clever enough to know what she wanted!

The Pancake

There was once a pancake that did not want to be eaten. So he jumped out of the pan and rolled away like a tyre, out of the door and into the world.

Soon a hare came up to him and called, "Thick, fat pancake, stay where you are, I want to eat you up!" "Hard luck," replied the pancake and rolled away.

Then a fox came up to him and said, "Thick, fat pancake, stay where you are, I want to eat you." But the pancake just scoffed and said, "Not likely." Then it rolled on its way again.

Then a pig came up to him and grunted, "Thick, fat pancake, I want to eat you." "Nothing doing," said the pancake, rolling away.

Then a child came up to the pancake and begged, "Thick, fat pancake, I'm so hungry!" "Now, that's different, you can eat me," said the pancake, "because you are more polite than all the others."

The Sewing Gnome

It was evening. The mother sighed as she sat down to do the sewing. She had lots of socks to darn and a pair of Roger's trousers to mend. When she opened her sewing basket she noticed something moving. To her great astonishment a tiny little gnome climbed out and asked, "Why do you sigh so?"

"Oh, it's because I'm forever having to sew up Roger's trousers and mend his socks and I'm sick of it! Who are you anyway?" she asked.

The little gnome laughed at this and said, "I've been living in this sewing box for ages. When you sighed tonight, I found it very upsetting so I've decided to help you. If you leave me a little bowl of my favourite chocolate pudding every night, I'll sew up all the trousers and socks."

The mother agreed, because it would mean an end to darning and sewing. She put out a bowl of chocolate pudding and the next morning she would find that all the trousers and socks were mended — and the chocolate pudding eaten!

This went on for a long time until the night Roger woke up feeling very thirsty. He got out of bed and went downstairs for a glass of water. As he walked through the lounge he spotted the bowl of chocolate pudding. He could not resist having a few mouthfuls and in no time he had eaten all the chocolate pudding that had been left out for the gnome. Then he drank a glass of water and went back to bed.

From then on, the gnome never did the sewing and darning. In fact Roger's mother had to do all the sewing and darning herself again. To this day she still does not know why the little gnome went away so suddenly.

Ladybirds Bring Luck

Once upon a time a chimney sweep and a clover leaf were having a discussion on how they could bring people good luck. A ladybird joined them because it, too, wanted to bring people good luck.

"Who are you then?" asked the chimney sweep, prodding the ladybird with one of his dirty fingers. He left a black mark on the ladybird's back. God thought that very beautiful and since then ladybirds have always had black spots on their backs.

The Flying Deckchair

Mr Williams sat down in his deckchair on the patio to relax after a hard day at the office. He lit his pipe and then lay back in the chair, closed his eyes and let his mind wander. He began to think about his next holiday in a far away land.

Suddenly the deckchair took off into the air, with Mr Williams still in the chair. They flew over hills and houses and finally they crossed the sea. Mr Williams thoroughly enjoyed his flight and leaned back in his chair to enjoy the view.

Then he realised that they were coming down to land in the middle of a desert. The sun was beating down and Mr William's forehead was covered in beads of sweat. Whilst he was wondering what to do, a Bedouin, wearing a police helmet and riding a camel, came up to him and asked, "Have you a ticket to show that you have paid to park here?"

Needless to say, Mr Williams did not have a ticket. Then the Bedouin policeman told Mr Williams off, and said, "What would happen if everybody in deckchairs was allowed to park wherever they wanted in the desert? I am therefore fining you." He took out a note book and began to write down Mr Williams' details.

At that point, the deckchair took off again and flew home with Mr Williams. He woke up with a start and had a throbbing headache. He resolved never to fall asleep in the sun again.

The Child and the Sun

The child said to the sun, "Why do you go away at night? When it's dark I can't play outside any more, and I have to go to bed. Why do you go away? What do you do behind the mountains?"

The sun replied, "Far behind the mountains, on the other side of the world, there are children just like you. They have slept all night long, and wait for me to wake them with my warm rays. They too, want to play outside just like you."

The child replied, "If that is so, then go now to the other children and shine on them. I'll go to bed and wait for you to wake me tomorrow morning."

So the sun replied, "Sweet dreams little one, until tomorrow morning!"

The Hungry Farmer

A long time ago, there was a farmer in Yugoslavia. One day he had to take his cow to the market to sell her. After he had completed his business he felt really hungry.

So he bought a bread roll, ate it quickly — but still felt hungry. He bought a second one, gobbled that up too — but still he felt hungry. Then he bought a sweet cracknel and when he had eaten it he felt full.

Feeling puzzled he scratched his head and thought, "What a silly fool I am! I needn't have bought those rolls, because as soon as I'd eaten the sweet cracknel I felt full! I should have bought the cracknel first and saved myself some money."

The Dachshund

Prince is a puppy who is full of energy and mischief. Recently he went on an expedition into the garden. He chased a butterfly and then he made a hole in the earth and threw up lots of soil!

Next he launched himself into the bushes. For a while he rummaged in the bushes, then he was still.

When he came out from the bushes, he had a bleeding nose. He had had an encounter with a hedgehog in the bushes. One thing is for certain, he won't ever meddle with such a prickly animal again!

A Dangerous Game

It was a very snowy Winter one year and the whole of our village lay deep in snow. We were a happy household. There were lots of us, two boys and three girls, and we loved to make up new games every day.

We loved to play in the snow more than anything else in the world. We would build huge snowmen and throw snowballs for hours on end. Once we even played at sliding down the roof of an old shed.

Then Keith decided to dive into the snow, just as if he were at the swimming baths. He dived headfirst into the snow and his head stuck, leaving his legs up in the air.

At first, we all burst out laughing. Then we saw that he was stuck and could not get his head out of the snow. Quickly, we fetched a shovel. We began to shovel him out of the snow.

It seemed ages before we got his head out from the snow. His face was blue with cold and he was gasping for breath. He was a little bit shaken but luckily that was all.

We realised just how dangerous this game had been, and made a promise never to play it again. In future we played less boisterous games in the snow, but always had lots of fun as long as it lasted.

The Flying Cat

The stork had built its nest on the chimney of the old farmhouse. When it stretched out its wings and flew into the sky, the cat looked at him enviously and thought, "If only I could fly too."

So the cat decided to try! It jumped onto the roof and then jumped off. As it jumped it stretched all four of its paws out as though they were wings, but it just landed with a bump on the ground!

"Flying is easy," said the cat to itself, "I need more practice at landing that's all!" And then he curled up on a bench and went to sleep in the warm sunshine.

Spring Flowers

The white snowdrop was asleep, beneath a layer of snow. The sun shone down and warmed the snowdrop with its rays.

At once, the snowdrop pushed its stem up to greet the sun. Then its little bell-like flowers began to ring and say, "Wake up, all you other flowers, Spring is here!"

The violet, the daisy and the yellow crocus all began to stir when they heard the sound of the snowdrop. Soon the tulip joined them. Then the snowdrop went back to sleep, all this growing had made it tired.

Brownie

Brownie is not the name of a dog in this story, but the name of a squirrel with a brown tail and a snow-white tummy.

For some time now he has been a regular visitor at our balcony and appears several times a day to stock up with food. We fill a flower pot with nuts and other squirrel foods, for Brownie our squirrel friend.

On one occasion Brownie rummaged so fiercely in the flower pot that he gave himself a shock by almost toppling it over and he had to take refuge in a nearby rose bush. But he soon got over his shock and returned to the balcony for more delicious food.

The School Satchel

"Can't you find your exercise book, Christopher?" asked the teacher when she saw him searching through his school satchel. "I'll have it in just a moment," replied Christopher, hastily.

"Wait, I'll help you," said the teacher, emptying all the contents of the bag onto the desk. It was unbelievable what Christopher had been storing in his bag. Out came torn up bits of paper, a broken ruler, a long piece of string, chestnuts, leaves, pencil stubs and — "What on earth is this?" asked the teacher, holding up a very mouldy sandwich.

"Christopher, if you do not want your sandwiches in the future, please either give them to someone else or throw them in the bin. Your school bag is not a dustbin!"

Christopher went bright red and thought to himself, "I'll never do that again!"

Pear Stalks

Trudy and Julian always spend their summer holidays at their grandparents' house in the country, where there's a massive garden with fruit trees to climb and long grass to walk bare foot through.

The pears had just become ripe and the two children began to eat as many as they could. As their grandmother was concerned about their health she ordered the children to show her the stalks of the pears they had eaten each day. Any more than ten between the two of them was not good for their digestion.

Every evening, Trudy and Julian would bring their Grandma just nine stalks and she would be content with this. Trudy said to her brother Julian, "Doesn't Grandma realise that there are pears which have fallen from the trees and do not have stalks?"

196

The Lazy Apprentice

There was once a baker's apprentice who was so lazy that he kept falling asleep when he was supposed to be working. "I'll have to do something about this," said the baker one day. The next time the apprentice fell asleep the baker discussed with the others how they should wake him.

The first baker suggested that they pour a jug of water over him. When they did this the apprentice just said, "Ooh, is it raining?" and went back to sleep.

The second baker suggested a good box on the ears. When the baker did this, the apprentice just woke briefly.

Then the third baker suggested that he shouted, "It's your day off today!" He did this and at once the apprentice jumped up and started to run home, but the baker stopped him just in time!

Losing a Tooth

"Mummy, I've got a wobbly tooth," called Jamie, showing his mother his loose tooth. "That will soon come out," said his mother.

"We could tie a piece of string around, fasten the other end to the door, so that the string will pull your tooth out," suggested Jamie's elder brother. But Jamie did not like that idea.

The next day, when Jamie came out of the nursery, his mother asked, "Where is your wobbly tooth?" Jamie looked at her in astonishment, then he felt the space with his tongue.

"Oh no, I must have swallowed the tooth when I had my sandwiches for lunch," he said.

"What a shame," said his mother, "I'd have liked to have saved your first milk tooth."

Un Unbelievable Tale

I once went down the street and saw a chimney sweep up on a roof. But he was so skinny that he fell down the chimney and had to be rescued from down below in the grate.

Then I continued on my way and saw a confectioner. He was so fat that he could not get through the doorway of his house and had to be lifted through a huge hole in the roof by crane.

Next I saw a fireman. He was so tall that he did not need a ladder to reach the fire, even if the fire was on the fifth floor of a building.

Later on, I met a postman. He rode along on his bicycle and threw the mail through open windows, because he was such a good shot!

What do you think of all these people? You've guessed—it was April Fool's Day!

The Two Clowns

Tony had been to the circus. When he came home his eyes were shining and he could not stop talking about all the acts he had seen. He had enjoyed the clown's act most of all.

He told his family for the third time, "Two clowns came into the ring. One was very tall and thin and the other one was short and fat. They wore baggy trousers, great big shoes and lots of bright make-up.

First the thin one took a water pistol and spurted water into the fat clown's mouth. Soon his tummy became fatter and fatter, the more water he swallowed. The tall clown then dropped the pistol on the floor. Then he pulled a plastic knife out of his trouser pocket and ran at the fat one with it. The fat one fell over as he ran and water spurted out from his tummy, just like a fountain!

Slowly, the fat clown's tummy went thinner, as all the water spurted out, and they stood up and everyone clapped and clapped until they had sore hands." That is what Tony told his family for the third time.

The Early Risers

The stork rises early in the morning. He shakes his feathers and then flies to the lake. The grass is still wet with dew and nothing is stirring.

Slowly, the long-necked stork paddles along the edge of the river bank. Then he dives down with his long beak and catches a frog. He swallows it. Next he catches a field mouse, two grasshoppers, a pair of caterpillars and lastly, a mole. He has stored enough by now so he flies back to his nest, where the baby storks are waiting for their breakfast.

Now father stork brings back all the food to feed his young. Mother stork joins them and helps feed the children. The storks fly to the lake several more times for food until the children have had enough to eat. Then mother and father stork put their beaks on their backs and have a well earned rest, just when everybody else is waking up!

The Three Wishes

When Winnie, the goblin, was returning home from blackberrying, it started to pour down with rain. So Winnie looked round for a place to shelter.

The fir tree called out to him, "Come and shelter under my branches, I'll protect you from the rain." Winnie gratefully accepted this kind offer and waited patiently under the fir tree for the rain to stop.

When the rain finally eased off, the goblin decided to set off for home. Just before he left, Winnie gave the fir tree three wishes. "If you say, Bright fir tree on the green grass, Winnie Goblin, grant me my wish. Then whatever you wish for will come true," said Winnie to the tree.

The fir tree was very glad to have three wishes. It had been longing for a new set of leaves for ages because the fir tree was tired of his sharp needles. So the tree uttered the

magic words and asked for a set of leaves made of glass. At once, it was covered in glass leaves which shimmered in the sunlight. But that night, the wind was so strong that it blew the glass leaves off the tree and they shattered into thousands of little pieces.

So then the little fir tree uttered the magic words and asked for leaves made of bright gold this time. Once again his wish was granted. The little tree was delighted to have such lovely golden leaves.

But that night, a robber came along and stole all the leaves. The little tree was heart broken, so it uttered the magic words and, as it had only one wish left, it decided not to take any more chances and asked for its old, green needles back. A few seconds later its old sharp needles came back. The little tree never complained about its needles again. It was quite satisfied with them.

Whatever Next!

There was once a Princess, who was always saying, "Whatever Next" and so everyone called her 'Whatever next', even though her real name was Melanie. When she grew up, her father, the King, said to her, "My dear child, it is time you chose a Prince for your husband. I am getting old and fed up with being the King."

The Princess just looked at him and said, "Whatever next!" The King took this to mean, "Alright, go ahead." Then he invited all the Princes from far and wide to the palace.

The Princes arrived in their hundreds to ask for the Princess's hand in marriage. She inspected them all and she said to each one of them, "Whatever next!" The Princes all took this phrase to mean, "No" and so they left the palace very disappointed.

In the end, the old King said, "My dear child, all your suitors have left and you have not chosen one of them to be your husband. You'll have to reign alone, for I'm abdicating." He then handed over his crown to the Princess. The Princess took the crown and remarked, "Whatever next!"

She was a good Queen and all her subjects loved her. Whenever a stranger arrived in the kingdom, and was told that the land was ruled by a woman, he would shake his head and say, "Whatever next!" At that, the subjects would nod their heads, and say, "Yes, that is what our Queen is called!"

Writing to Santa

Felix is seven years old. This year he is writing to Santa Claus by himself for the very first time. When he had finished his list, he handed his letter over to his mother to read.

Felix put an electric train, a toy car, a pair of skis, an exciting book, a box of magic tricks, paints, bow and arrow, boxing gloves and lots of sweets on his list! His mother shook her head in disbelief, "Don't you think you're asking for rather a lot?" she asked. But Felix did not think so.

He waited impatiently for Christmas. On Christmas morning, he woke up very early and crept downstairs to open his presents. Sure enough, he found them under the tree. He opened them all, but was disappointed when he saw that he had only been given a pair of skis and a box of magic tricks — and a letter.

It read, "Dear Felix, there were so many presents on your list that I have shared them out with three other children. I hope that is what you had in mind. Merry Christmas and a Happy New Year." It was signed Santa Claus.

Felix felt ashamed for being so greedy.

Bill and Ben

"Hey, Bill," called Ben, "what are you doing here, what's that you've got in your hands?" "It's an earth worm — a big, fat, juicy one!" replied Bill.

"Yuck! a worm, throw it away," said Ben who hated worms. "Don't you know that worms are very good for the soil?" said Bill. "No, I didn't know that and I'm not very interested anyway," retorted Ben. "Well, that's why I'm putting him back in the soil," said Bill.

"Good," replied Ben, "because for a moment I thought we were going to have worms for breakfast!"

The Sandman

Tonight Daddy is putting his young son to bed. "Quickly now, get down under the blankets, because the Sandman will be here in a minute," said the boy's father. "Who is the Sandman?" asked the little boy. "He's a little man with a sack on his back full of the finest sand there is," replied the father.

"What does he do with the sand then?" asked the little boy. "The Sandman comes up to the children just before they go to sleep and gently sprinkles grains of sand into their eyes to make them fall asleep," explained the little boy's father.

"Aah, now I know why I always have to wipe away the sleepyness from my eyes in the morning!" exclaimed the little boy.

Lazybones and the Sun

The sun sends its rays to the earth in the morning to wake up Lazybones! The rays tickle him gently on the nose and behind the ears. But Lazybones just stirs slightly, turns over and carries on sleeping. The sun then wakes the cock who crows, "Cock-a-doodle-do!" But still Lazybones does not wake.

Then the sun wakes the dog who begins to bark, "Wuff, wuff!" But still Lazybones does not stir. So the sun wakes the bells which ring, "Ding, dong!" And still Lazybones sleeps.

Then the sun wakes the boy's mother. She gets up, pulls the covers off Lazybones and calls, "Wakey, wakey, time to get up, the sun is shining!" And at last Lazybones wakes up!

The Photograph

"Hey, Bill, I'm going to take a photograph of you for Grandma. She has been wanting one for ages now," said Ben. "Great!" replied Bill. "Should I go and comb my hair first?"

"No, you're okay just as you are," replied Ben. "Stay still and smile — 'Cheese'!" Click, Ben takes the photograph. "Hey Ben, will it come out alright, it looks as though you have left the lens cap on?" said Bill. "What!" yelled Ben. "Left the lens cap on? Oh no!" he cried in horror.

So poor Grandma had to make do with a very dark photograph of Bill. In fact she could hardly make him out at all. Ben made himself feel better by telling Grandma that he had taken the picture in the dark!